THE AWAKENING

THE FRIESSEN LEGACY

THE OUTSIDER SERIES

LORHAINNE ECKHART

ISBN-13: 978-1990590900

Give feedback on the book at:
lorhainneeckhart@hotmail.com

Twitter: @LEckhart
Facebook: AuthorLorhainneEckhart

Printed in the U.S.A

THE FRIESSEN FAMILY SERIES
READING ORDER:

The Outsider Series

The Forgotten Child (Brad and Emily)
A Baby And A Wedding
Fallen Hero (Andy, Jed, and Diana)
The Search
The Awakening (Andy and Laura)
Secrets (Jed and Diana)
Runaway (Andy and Laura)
Overdue
The Unexpected Storm (Neil and Candy)
The Wedding (Neil and Candy)

The Friessens: A New Beginning

The Deadline (Andy and Laura)
The Price to Love (Neil and Candy)
A Different Kind of Love (Brad and Emily)
A Vow of Love, A Friessen Family Christmas

The Friessens

The Reunion
The Bloodline (Andy & Laura)
The Promise (Diana & Jed)
The Business Plan (Neil & Candy)
The Decision (Brad & Emily)
First Love (Katy)
Family First
Leave the Light On
In the Moment
In the Family: A Friessen Family Christmas
In the Silence
In the Stars
In the Charm
Unexpected Consequences
It Was Always You
The First Time I Saw You
Welcome to My Arms
Welcome to Boston (A Paige & Morgan Short Story)
I'll Always Love You
Ground Rules
A Reason to Breathe
You Are My Everything
Anything For You
The Homecoming
When They Were Young (Link included FREE with The
Homecoming)
Stay Away From My Daughter
The Bad Boy
A Place of Our Own
The Visitor

All About Devon
Long Past Dawn
How to Heal a Heart
Keep Me In Your Heart

The Friessen Family

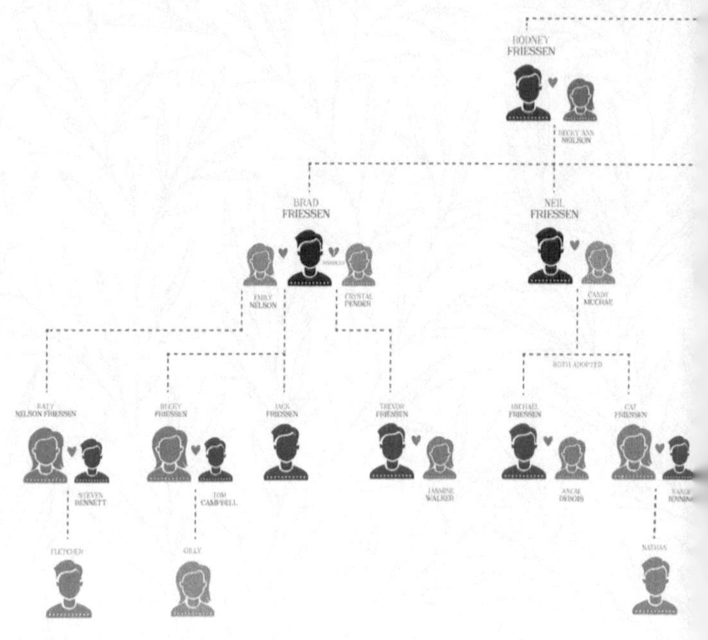

The Outsider Series

THE FORGOTTEN CHILD	BRAD & EMILY
A BABY AND A WEDDING	BRAD & EMILY &
FALLEN HERO	JED, DIANA & ANDY
THE SEARCH	JED, DIANA & ANDY
THE AWAKENING	ANDY & LAURA

The Outsider Series

SECRETS	DIANA & JED *with the entire Friessen Family*
RUNAWAY	ANDY & LAURA
OVERDUE	JED & DIANA
THE UNEXPECTED STORM	NEIL & CANDY
THE WEDDING	NEIL & CANDY *and the entire Friessen Family*

The Friessens: A New Beginning

THE DEADLINE	ANDY & LAURA
THE PRICE TO LOVE	NEIL & CANDY
A DIFFERENT KIND OF LOVE	BRAD & EMILY
A VOW OF LOVE	THE ENTIRE
A FRIESSEN FAMILY CHRISTMAS	FRIESSEN FAMILY

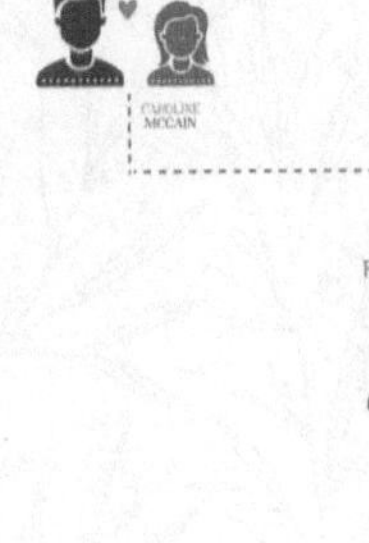

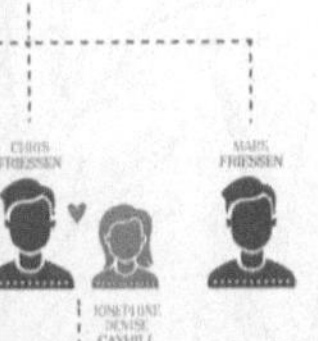

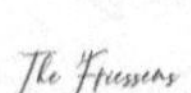

The Friessens

THE ENTIRE FRIESSEN FAMILY	LEAVE THE LIGHT ON	KATY & STEVEN
ANDY & LAURA	IN THE MOMENT	BECKY & TOM
JED & DIANA	IN THE FAMILY, *A Friessen Family Christmas*	THE ENTIRE FRIESSEN FAMILY
NEIL & CANDY	IN THE SILENCE	CAT & XANDER
BRAD & EMILY	IN THE STARS	DANNY & EVIE
KATY & STEVEN	IN THE CHARM	CHRIS & JD
KATY & STEVEN	UNEXPECTED CONSEQUENCES	CHRIS & JD

The Friessens

IT WAS ALWAYS YOU	KATY & STEVEN
THE FIRST TIME I SAW YOU	GABRIEL & ELIZABETH
WELCOME TO MY ARMS	CHELSEA & ALARIC
WELCOME TO BOSTON	PAIGE & MORGAN
I'LL ALWAYS LOVE YOU	JEREMY
GROUND RULES	JEREMY & TIFFY
A REASON TO BREATHE	TREVOR & JASMINE
YOU ARE MY EVERYTHING	MICHAEL & ANGIE
ANYTHING FOR YOU	A CAT & XANDER NOVELLA
THE HOMECOMING	THE ENTIRE FRIESSEN FAMILY

A young woman who's lost everything, and the wealthy rancher who must choose between his family's power and his conscience to help her.

In THE AWAKENING, Laura, a young single mother is barely making ends meet working as a maid at the Friessen mansion. Until one day she is fired, the next day she is evicted, and two days later her son is taken away.

Wealthy rancher Andy Friessen can have any woman he wants, but when Laura is fired by his mother over something he was responsible for, well his conscience gets the better of him and he steps in to help. The problem is when he goes looking for Laura he not only discovers she's been living in her car, but the state took her child away.

With Andy standing beside her through a courtroom fiasco, they must fight together to regain custody of her son.

CHAPTER I

"Get this god-awful tree out of here!" Andy shouted as he stormed into the grand library, his dark hide boots barely making a sound on the rich scarlet carpet as he cut a path toward his large mahogany desk. The library was his domain, a showpiece of the Friessen mansion. It was a very masculine room, filled with browns and reds, dark wood, leather chairs, oil paintings worth more than the estate, a room Andy had appointed as his office.

"Sir, your mother ordered this tree and left instructions for it to be set up and decorated in this very room," Laura, a very young, pretty blond maid responded without glancing Andy's way. She pursed her soft red lips and continued to hang bright green ornaments on the vibrant white tree.

Andy slid his large hand under a branch of the Douglas-fir. "I didn't know that fir trees grew white. What, did you have this dyed?"

This time, the maid glanced at Andy with those sea-green eyes, wearing the ugly maid uniform that hung like a grain sack from what he could only imagine was a slim body underneath. It was the most unflattering getup, with a starched collar and buttoned up to her chin. And, of course, Andy being Andy, he couldn't help wondering how she'd look in something low cut, slinky, and black. Preferably something that fit her like a second skin and showed off the generous bust he was pretty sure was buried under that stiff black cloth.

Maybe she'd guessed where his mind drifted, as her face colored and her eyes sharpened into narrow slits. "Your mother made sure all the trees were colored specifically for each room. The one in the living room, you'll be happy to know, is green." She averted her gaze and started yanking the ornaments off, pine needles dropping to the blood-red carpet, which was the only thing in this house he'd had a say in.

"So, Laura, is it?" Andy didn't know why, but there was something about this girl who'd been working in his household since the spring, when he'd first seen her cowering and petrified in the hallway the day Jed disappeared. His cousin, whom he loved dearly, was married to Diana, a woman who haunted his dreams but would never be his. Andy and Diana had worked together to find an injured Jed, thrown from the stallion he had been training up toward blue meadow, and Diana had added to the excitement by going into labor, delivering their baby boy, Danny, Andy's godson, that same night. He'd seen Laura in town shortly after holding a little boy's hand, and he'd since wondered who he was. She didn't look old enough to have children, as she appeared fresh out of high school. But, then again, he never asked, because he, unlike his father, didn't become personal with the staff, especially attractive young things who worked for him, because that wasn't okay. It was morally wrong, and he was having a hard time remembering what the other reason was. Ah, yes, sexual harassment.

"Yes?" The girl was staring at him with those big green eyes. He'd swear they were tinged with flecks of gold, which only illuminated her silky pale skin. She had not a spot of makeup on, but then, she didn't need it. She had soft skin that just begged to be touched, and, frankly, Andy was tired of all those women who caked on the pounds of makeup like a mask just to hop in their cars to go to the store.

"Sorry, been distracted lately. I was just wondering how things are going, if you're being treated okay. Do you like working here?"

Damn, that wasn't what he really wanted to know, but he had to remind himself again that she worked for him, for his family. As he thought about it, he didn't rightly know who had hired her, but the sizeable staff in the house and on the grounds was generally handled by Jules, the head housekeeper, a plump older lady who'd been with the family since Andy was in short pants. Andy wondered, too, if the deep lines on Jules' face and the thick gray in her hair were a result of him and the wily pranks he had played on her as a child.

Laura dropped her gaze again, her cheeks tinting a hint of pink as she boxed up the ornaments. "Everything's fine, sir." She said it so abruptly and carried on as if trying to ignore him, and that irritated the hell out of him. She worked for him. She'd damn well give him her full attention, and he'd see to that now.

"Laura, you work for me. So when I ask you something, I expect your attention and a truthful answer," he growled.

Her face colored a brighter red, and she glanced back at him warily. Andy, being as astute as he was, didn't miss the hint of dislike that she was doing her damnedest to hide, but it was a piss-poor attempt.

"You're right about one thing: I do work for you, but you don't own me, and you don't know me well enough to tell whether I gave you a truthful answer. So again, I'll repeat it, everything's fine, sir," she responded in a tone that was pure business. This time, she didn't look away as she continued to blush furiously, her lips pursed and trembling slightly as she stared up at him.

"If that's all, sir, I'll finish taking down these ornaments and haul the tree out of here." Again, she stared him down with those green eyes, resembling a very enticing witch, a witch he wouldn't mind getting to know a little better.

Andy uncrossed his arms and moved to his desk, pulling out his leather chair and sitting down. He propped both his booted feet on the sleek polished wood top of the desk, crossing his legs at the ankles, and watched her, lacing his fingers behind his head. She seemed startled, as her eyes widened. Maybe she expected him to leave.

"Carry on" was all he said.

She took a moment to collect herself before continuing to yank ornaments from the branches as if she were being timed. Pine needles flew everywhere. She was in a hurry, all right, not just to finish but to get the hell away from him.

When she bent over in that god-awful uniform, the dress rode up her thighs, and he was treated to a view of her shapely legs. She was tiny, her head wouldn't have topped his shoulders—and nervous as hell, too. He could see her trembling. Although not obvious, it was something he sensed, just like he sensed she wasn't thinking about the poor tree. She was just ripping those damn ornaments from that tacky tree as fast as she could, and he had no doubt she'd bolt as soon as the last one was off. For the life of him, he'd never experienced a woman running from him. This was intriguing, or it would have been if he didn't feel so irritated by the fact that it bothered him. Women didn't do that, not to Andy Friessen. Women found any ridiculous excuse to find a way to be around him. In town, at the store, dropping items, a purse, a bag—one woman even unbuttoned her blouse to expose a generous amount of indecent skin before crossing the street to him, putting an extra sway into each step. He'd never had a problem finding a woman for anything. The fact was that most of them bored him to tears, except Diana, his cousin's wife. And she'd never be his.

"Oh, no!"

Andy was so deep in thought, he only glimpsed Laura as she took a header into the white Christmas tree, and it came crashing down, all twelve feet of tinted fir needles, with a whoosh and scrape of wood. Something thumped hard, and glass shattered.

Andy jumped up, slamming his feet on the thick carpet as he raced around the desk. Laura was tangled in the tree. Her dress had ridden up, showing the elastic of her old-lady panties. The only thing Andy could think was what a waste they were on such a lovely round, curvy butt.

"Are you okay?" Andy reached down and lifted Laura as he would a child, and he sat her on the edge of the desk.

"Mr. Friessen, whatever is going on in here?" Jules, the older, graying, plump housekeeper who ran the estate, hurried into the library but was stopped by the downed tree. She slapped both hands to her round cheeks and shrieked. Shattered ornaments, bits of fir needles, and broken branches were strewn across the plush red carpet and the sofa table. The huge tree had knocked over one of the leather chairs and the bar that had been moved to the other side of the room to make room for it. Decanters and liquor bottles lay on their sides, the crystal shattered, liquor pooling and seeping into the carpet. Laura sat perched on the edge of Andy's desk, white fir needles sticking out of her blond hair, though they were hard to see unless he really looked. Her neat bun had drooped, and her hair hung in an untidy mess. Her entire expression had turned into that of a lost young girl, as if she couldn't believe what she'd done.

"Oh my God!" Caroline, his mother, shouted as she strode in with all the elegance of a queen, dressed in a deep green silk knee-length dress that hugged her every curve and showed what an attractive woman she still was. Her shoulder-length light hair was impeccably groomed, and when she stopped beside Jules, her mouth opened as if she couldn't think of what to say. Then her shrewd gaze landed on Laura, and her pale blue eyes turned frosty and unforgiving. "What a mess you've made, girl."

Even Andy was taken aback by the iciness of her tone, and he didn't miss the way Laura cringed, like a dowdy school girl. Hell, Andy had cowered under his mother as a little boy when she'd have one of her tantrums, generally after he'd broken some useless and really expensive trinket of hers.

"I'm so sorry, ma'am. I tripped, but I'll... c-clean this up," she stuttered and pressed her small hand to her throat.

Andy narrowed his eyes and watched Caroline, as she appeared to just be winding up for one of her many tantrums. As far back as Andy could remember, his mother had never shown an ounce of empathy toward anyone, not even her own child. And this time was no different. She glared at Laura with as much feeling as a viper and the energy of one that was about to strike, and then she surveyed the damage, the disarray, and the mess with a swift, well-organized glance. Lifting her chin and straightening her back, she spoke clearly: "The damage will come out of your last check. Jules, see that she's escorted off the property within the next five minutes." She looked over to Laura. "Do not ever return. If you do, the proper authorities will be called."

Andy jerked his gaze from his mother to Laura's wide eyes, now filled with tears. He could tell she was struggling to hold it together, as she appeared to have trouble swallowing. "Mother, it was an accident. You're being a bit hasty. For God's sake, it's just a stupid tree, and I ordered her to get it out of here. I made it clear to you before that if you want to decorate the rest of the house, it's fine—just stay out of my office," Andy said to his mother, but Caroline, who could be so prickly at times, stood unbending and in fact raised one eyebrow.

"Anderson, the tree stays. The girl goes. I have guests arriving for our annual Christmas party. You'll have your office back after Christmas. Jules, the girl, get rid of her." She literally snapped her fingers, and Jules jumped, saying, "Yes, Mrs. Friessen," and motioning frantically at Laura.

Caroline didn't stay but strode from the room, the heels of her silver pumps clicking across the marble floor of the grand entry and down two steps to an exquisite living room, with fancy white trim, which was decorated in peach and gold, floor-to-ceiling windows, and velvety white carpet. A twelve-foot cream-colored Christmas tree was also decorated to perfection with gold, silver, and red.

Caroline walked as if she were in a beauty contest, head

high, striding to a small round dinette set where one of the maids had set a china tea service. Caroline had to know he was following her, but she ignored Andy, which was a skill she'd perfected years before. It was amazing—his mother broke the mold in snobbery, and he'd never met anyone who could look right through him and choose whether to see him quite like his mother could.

She brushed aside the white napkin that had been folded over the gold china cup, pouring tea and adding a generous amount of milk. She sipped and picked up the day timer sitting on the antique glass-top desk by the window. She never glanced up as she sat in the white leather chair that was matched to all the furnishings in the room. "Is there something you would like, Andy? As I said, I have a million things to do today to organize this household and be ready in time for the party." She glanced up at him and pasted on one of her practiced smiles that always charmed the senators.

"Mother, I am not going to continue butting heads with you. What you did, firing Laura just now, wasn't okay. For God's sake, she didn't deserve to be treated like that," Andy stated, rather annoyed, and gestured toward the library before setting his hands on his hips. He stood in front of her desk, glaring down at her until she slowly, with the control of a seasoned politician, set down her tea and folded her hands neatly on the desk, eyeing him coolly.

"Anderson, this is my house. Therefore, the servants work for me, and I will decide how they are treated and who stays and who goes, not you." She picked up her cup again and sipped, then gave him one of her disapproving looks. "Laura, really? Already on a first-name basis? In some ways, you really are like your father." She said it with such disdain, and the fact that she had alluded to the possibility of him playing hanky-panky with the maid irritated the hell out of him, even though, less than ten minutes before, he had been imagining Laura dressed down in something completely indecent and doing all kinds of lewd things with him. He often wondered what kind of sixth sense his mother had for the perverse. But then, she had to, being married to his dad, Todd, who had the uncanny ability to sniff out a new mistress as soon as he tired of one, just to keep his interests alive and his bed warm. His father could be like a hound dog when he was hot on the trail of a new scent. Andy liked to think that trait was Todd's alone, and he would ram his fist in the face of anyone who accused him of being a scoundrel, toying with women's hearts and tossing them away when he was done. There was a very big difference between Andy having any woman he wanted and Andy being like Todd Friessen.

So he bared his teeth and growled at his mother, because he was damn tired of cleaning up after his father and putting up with his mother's arrogance. "You know what's absolutely amazing? How you treat people and have for years, just by snapping your fingers and expecting everyone to jump, with no care to anyone's feelings. You and Dad are so much the same, it's absolutely terrifying."

"I am not like that..." Caroline sputtered, but Andy didn't let her finish.

"You are exactly like him. You believe everyone is replaceable and have little care for anyone's feelings. Dad, with every woman he beds. You, with the servants, how you treat everyone. You know what? I'm done cleaning up. I've got my own life to live." Andy was shouting, but Caroline hardened her expression better than any snake he'd ever met. When she did that, even Andy felt a rush of worry, because the woman was the only one who could yank the rug out from under him—there was no way to know what she was thinking.

"I've invited Alexis Johnston. You remember, the senator's daughter. She just graduated from Stanton, and I told the senator that you'd be her escort for the party. He's counting on you. Don't disappoint me, Andy. Whatever you're doing with your maids, keep it in the closet, where it belongs." She issued the order as if she expected him to fall into line, then picked up a stack of envelopes and started filing through them.

Andy laughed so hard that tears came to his eyes. His mother really was a piece of work. "You must have been drinking or something, because you don't ever order me to do anything. You certainly are not fixing me up with any woman." He ground his teeth together before growling, "Not ever, Mother." He could feel the irritation biting the back of his neck as he strode out, and he wanted nothing more than to ram his fist into a wall.

But he didn't, and he wasn't even out of the room when Caroline spoke in a loud, clear voice: "Oh, I think you will, since Senator Johnson is on the very committee that your cousin Jed approached for funding for his therapeutic riding."

Andy's blood chilled, and all the fiery anger he had been containing moments ago was replaced with an array of worry he hadn't experienced in a long time. Only his mother could knock him over and leave him absolutely speechless. He turned slowly to meet the sharp gleam in the woman's ice-blue eyes. A woman who had given birth to him, a woman he had no doubt would sell him down the river for the right offer if it was in her best interest.

"Yes, the senator and I had quite a chat about how tight funding is now, with the national debt this country carries and how selective any new programming must be. It's quite a project, really, that your cousin is starting with that Claremont he married. I mean, really, the senator can't be providing funding to just anyone." Her face was hard as stone, not a flicker of emotion. He wondered for a moment if she had a bone of feeling in her body.

"Diana is her name, and she was a Fulton when she married Jed. She never deserved to be treated that way as a child. Diana and Jed are good people, Mother. You stay away from them, and stay out of Jed's business." He ground out each word, reminding himself she was his mother and, no matter what, it was never okay to strangle one's own mother. But he also knew his mother never made threats; she insinuated, she dug, and she destroyed those she didn't like, and she never gave any warning. *The Art of War*, she could have written it. But Caroline, being Caroline, always had an agenda, and it was never wise to let her know what mattered to him, because she would use it. Andy had learned that the hard way over the years. When he was twelve, she'd gotten rid of his pony, Chantelle, the one he'd whispered all his dreams to. Just because he refused to go to some fancy boys' school in England that her father, uncles, and brothers had all attended.

"I told the senator you'll pick up his daughter when she flies in tomorrow. She'll be staying here at the estate."

This time, Andy walked away before he could respond, the fury pouring out of him with each step. Back in the library, two servants were righting the downed Christmas tree, and another scrawny maid in a sack-like dress was on her knees, cleaning up the shattered glass and decanters. Another one was scrubbing the liquor seeping into the carpet.

"Get out!" Andy roared, and each of them stopped what they were doing and left.

Andy was breathing hard as if he'd run across the estate. He jammed his fingers in his hair as he paced and froze in front of the large window, watching as Laura was escorted down the front driveway.

CHAPTER 2

Laura Parnell couldn't stop shaking. She'd never felt such bone-deep humiliation as when Mrs. Friessen fired her. Jules had shown her the door, scolding her the entire way through the mansion. Adding to her shame, she then forced her to stand at the back door with her coat on while the head housekeeper summoned two men, neither of whom had a sliver of interest in her predicament. When they arrived with Jules five minutes later, Laura had been unable to swallow and was shaking, an agony twisting up her stomach. She wondered if she might vomit right in the doorway. No matter how she tried, her brain just wouldn't grasp how bad the situation really was.

Stan, a young, blond man she recognized as Mrs. Friessen's driver, grabbed her elbow roughly and said, "Let's go. Start walking, girl." Ed, the burly gardener, flanked her other side, walking her up the long, slate-gray driveway for half a mile to the highway. It was Ed who muttered, "Take my advice, deary. Don't set foot back here or the sheriff will be called." Then they stood and watched her, and for the first time Laura felt real fear.

Laura could only nod as a tear slipped down her cheek and she started walking home. She usually shared a ride with Sue, one of the other maids who worked at the estate, but there wasn't a chance in hell that Sue asked if she could leave and drive Laura home, and it wasn't as if Laura could have asked her anyway. When Jules had ordered Laura to stand by the door and wait, not touching anything, Sue pretended she didn't know her and ducked her head, continuing to peel potatoes in the kitchen. Laura hadn't expected Sue to go to bat for her. She hadn't expected her to ignore her, either, as she stood terrified by the back door as Jules searched out the two men. It hurt, and even though she knew Sue needed the job, so did Laura. She wondered if there was such a thing as simple human compassion inside anyone anymore.

Laura pulled up the collar of her thin blue coat. The zipper had broken, so she could only fasten it closed with the metal snaps. At one time, it had probably been a nice coat, but at least it was a coat, and the price was right at the second-hand store. It did little to stop the chill from seeping into her bones, though, as she started shivering. She was no more dressed for a stroll downtown than the five-mile walk back to North Lakewood. The Friessen estate was just outside the small town, which didn't seem that far when driving but was a long way when you were walking. Even though she wore sensible shoes for work, they were not made for the wet highway. Though it had stopped raining for the moment, the wind blew, and the thick, dark clouds overhead were threatening to unleash one hell of a storm. Laura just hoped it would hold off until she made it back to town.

A few cars passed, going the other way, but no one stopped. She'd just rounded a bend when she heard a car behind her. Her feet were numb, and her stockings were soaked and muddy. She shuffled over further on the shoulder and felt tears of relief. The moment she saw the shiny blue pickup, the fancy one she'd seen Andy drive, she froze. She could feel his eyes lock on her, and she couldn't help but duck her head in embarrassment. Of all people, why did it have to be Andy who stopped? He'd witnessed one of the most embarrassing moments of her life, but then, he was partly responsible. Laura could barely function around him; he was far too good looking, and the power oozed off him. Every time he walked into the room, Laura felt as if she'd been plugged into a socket, and she would struggle not to trip over both her feet as she hurried away from him. This was exactly what had happened when she took a header into the Christmas tree, knocking it down. She also knew he watched her in a way that was entirely indecent, and she could feel the heat of his gaze burning into her. His father did, too, but she went out of her way to avoid Todd Friessen. She'd heard all the rumors of how he played with women, and she couldn't help thinking the apple didn't fall too far from the tree with Andy. She had no plans of being anyone's whore.

He pulled to the side of the road and got out. He overwhelmed her with his size as he stepped around the front of the truck, and she really disliked having to look up at him. She shoved her bare hands in her coat pockets, unsure of what to say or do. This was about as bad as it could get today. Then she wondered, how did one go about being rescued?

"You're walking?" He swept his gaze downward, taking in everything from her bare legs to her shoes and her thin coat. "Get in. I'll give you a ride." He didn't wait for her to answer but pressed his hand into the small of her back, hustling her to his truck.

Laura felt as if her brain had gone to mush, as she couldn't for the life of her think of anything intelligent to say as Andy closed the passenger door. When he slid in under the steering wheel, his eyes lingered on her, and she felt her cheeks burning. She needed to do something but, short of jumping out and freezing, she couldn't think of anything. She swallowed her discomfort and grabbed the seat belt, jamming it in. Thankfully, Andy started the truck, driving toward town. It would be short and painless. They'd be there in no time, he could drop her off at the corner, and she'd never have to see him again.

"Where do you live?"

She stared out the windshield and pointed straight ahead. "Just outside downtown. You can just drop me off at the corner by the school. There's a daycare. I need to pick up my son."

She didn't know why, but she didn't want Andy to take her home or know she lived in the tiny basement suite of a piece-of-shit rundown old house. She kept her space neat and tidy, but from the outside it didn't look like much. An older lady, who chain-smoked lived upstairs and wasn't great at keeping up the front yard. Which would always be the first impression anyone had of the place: overgrown weeds, long grass, and unkempt bushes. An untidy mess. Laura looked after the backyard, which was a sharp contrast to the front, but then, people didn't see the back, so they just assumed it was her. They judged her, and she hated that feeling. She'd rather Andy didn't see it at all. It irritated her further that she cared what he thought, because it shouldn't matter. He shouldn't matter. The fact was that she was just tired of everyone looking down their noses at her, which they had done throughout her entire teenage pregnancy, and it hurt. Didn't people get that?

"So, do you have family around?"

She could feel his gaze burning into her as she stared straight ahead. He waited for her to answer. Why couldn't he just drive and ignore her? It hurt to talk; she didn't think she could get her throat to work. She needed to crawl into bed and pull the covers up over her head.

"No," she responded in a voice she didn't recognize, and she was grateful when Andy pulled into the parking lot of the school. "Here's good." She pointed to the concrete steps, but he didn't stop until he pulled into a parking spot and shut off the engine.

"You have a boyfriend or husband at home?"

"No." That was the last thing she wanted to talk about: Tyler, Gabriel's father, who she hadn't seen since she was six months pregnant and had been forced to drop out of school. He'd treated her as if she had something he might catch, running the other way every time he saw her. Yeah, she got that message loud and clear, but it didn't stop the ache that burned a giant hole where her heart had once beat.

Laura shut her eyes and took a deep breath to still the shaking in her hands. She couldn't go in looking the mess she felt. Andy strode around to her side, so Laura scrambled for her door handle and yanked it, pushing her door open, clearing her throat to thank him and then slink away up those cracked concrete stairs and into that old building. But Andy slid his hand over the top of her door as she slid out, and he stood right in her space, holding out his hand for her. She just stared and didn't think, setting her hand in his, which was so warm and big that it all but swallowed hers up. Touching him did little to calm her, and she pulled her hand away, clutching her raggedy purse because she needed to do something, as she was acutely embarrassed from his touch.

"Well, thank you for the ride. I can walk from here."

Andy didn't move. He was still right in front of her, blocking her way. "I'll drive you and your son home."

She wondered in that moment, as a rush of tingling heat left her face, whether all the color had left with it. She was, after all, no good at hiding her feelings. She didn't want Andy's help, and she definitely didn't want him driving her and her son home, but when he raised dark eyebrows over those hard blue eyes, she knew he wasn't going away, so she dropped her gaze and started walking inside the old school and down the inside steps to the daycare in the basement. She knocked on the glass window. A dark-haired lady smiled and pressed a button that unlocked the door. Andy was right behind her; she could feel his heat as if he pressed into her, but he wasn't touching her at all. He was right in her space, right behind her, holding the door for her as she stepped in. She didn't have to look up at him to know that he was taking every part of this daycare in, from the overcrowded conditions, with too many kids and not enough workers, to the bargain basement toys. But this was all she could afford. Again, it bothered her what he must be thinking. She was tired of people getting into her business and knowing too much about her.

"You're here early. I wasn't expecting you until this evening?" Peggy, the short, dark-haired woman in her late forties who owned the daycare, glanced at Andy. "Hello, Mr. Friessen. This is a surprise." Peggy appeared more than interested and did nothing to hide her curiosity as she glanced from Laura to Andy. Great. Laura could almost see the wheels spinning in her mind. She was about to be the flavor of the week—the gossip would be unbearable.

"I'm picking up Gabriel now," Laura said. She could feel Andy's eyes burning into her as he stood behind her. In fact, he stepped closer, and she knew he was taking in the entire place. He didn't touch her, but he may as well have put his hand on her shoulder. It was almost the same, by how close he was standing.

"I'm still going to have to charge you for the full day, you understand," Peggy stated quite loudly, sounding annoyed. Laura knew the woman wasn't about to let the matter drop. Peggy strode across the concrete floor to the corner where Gabriel was playing with a box of Lego bricks. Gabriel didn't look up when she knelt beside him. Peggy tossed the Legos into the box, and Gabriel started fussing. Then she took his hand. Laura was sweating because Peggy was about as discreet as a two-dollar hooker. She called out to Laura from across the room, so everyone could hear, "Will Gabriel be back tomorrow morning, same time?"

Laura swallowed, her face burning by the time Peggy handed Gabriel over. She knelt down and zipped up Gabriel's faded red coat. Her four-year-old little boy said not a word. "No, not tomorrow." She kept her eyes on that zipper and on Gabriel, hoping Peggy would just get the message and drop it.

"Oh, is it my mistake? I have you down for tomorrow. Five days this week. Did I mix up the days?"

Why, at this moment, couldn't the floor just open up and swallow her? Peggy was marching to a big drawer by the sink where she kept all her business records and every-thing personal about all the parents who brought their kids to this daycare, and she yanked out her day timer just to prove to Laura she was right. Laura wished Andy were anywhere but there. She wanted to ask him to leave, but that would mean she'd have to turn around and face him, and she couldn't do that as she stood frozen like an awkward teenager. As she stood up, her legs were trembling so hard her knees knocked together.

"No, he won't be back this week." Laura nibbled on her lip, feeling her face heat.

Peggy dropped her pen and sighed, letting Laura know she was irritated. "You do realize you still have to pay for the week. As I've reserved that spot for you, others were turned away, so you may as well let him come. You were given our outlined policy when you enrolled here. I will not be out any money, Laura. We have a very strict cancellation policy...."

Laura cut her off. "You will be paid, but Gabriel won't be coming. Come on, honey. Let's go," she snapped, reaching for Gabriel's hand and starting toward the door, brushing past Andy.

"How much does she owe?" Andy asked in a tone she'd heard him use many a time on the phone.

Laura froze mid-step beside Andy. She couldn't believe this was happening. She stared up at him just as he unzipped a pocket inside his black leather coat and yanked out his wallet. She wanted to yell "No, stop!" but she couldn't get her tongue to move, and she watched in horror as Andy lifted what looked like several hundred dollars out and dropped it on the counter in front of Peggy. The woman moved her mouth to say something as her round cheeks flushed a nice rosy pink and she picked up all the bills.

"And—Mr. Friessen, I can pay my own way." Laura had finally found her voice, but stumbled when she almost used his first name. She'd never addressed him at all, only ever responding to his orders. She, unlike the rest of the staff at the mansion, never addressed him, period, and she went out of her way to avoid him at all costs. So, of course, she was stumped on what to call him now, because his actions now went way beyond employer–employee. She didn't know what the hell this was.

"Let's go" was all he said in response. His tone was sharp and dismissive, and he reached around her and yanked open the door, his hand holding the top so she had to scoot under his arm. She didn't miss the way Peggy watched in a way that made Laura know that as soon as she stepped out that door, the daycare owner would be on the phone to half a dozen of her friends, giving the latest on Andy and Laura. It would be horrible. Laura wouldn't be able to show her face anywhere. It was hard enough now, as people talked. What made it worse was that she'd heard some of the talk around town about the Friessen men, how they used women to warm their beds. Those women were called tarts, tramps, and sluts, and she didn't want to be tarred with that brush.

Laura hurried up the steps and outside to his truck. His heavy footsteps were right behind her and pounded with the beat of her heart. She could feel him and wasn't sure if she was feeling irritation, annoyance, or regret at what he'd done.

"You know, we could walk the rest of the way. I'm not far from here. You don't have to drive us." She was positive her voice squeaked, and she didn't look at him, but he placed his hand on her lower back as if hurrying her along and yanked open the passenger door.

"No, I'll drive you." He held the door open for her and then stepped around her and Gabriel, sliding her seat forward and pulling a strap in the back middle seat down.

Laura was surprised when it opened into a car seat, not something she'd thought of.

Andy then reached for Gabriel, who she'd lifted into her arms, and that was when she tightened her hold on her son. It was instinctive, and he must have noticed, because he said, "I'm not going to hurt him, Laura. Let me fasten him in."

Laura glanced at her son, wondering if he'd let Andy touch him. She started to lift Gabriel to Andy, and Andy took it from there, reaching for him. The boy's eyes went wide, and he whined, reaching his tiny arms out to Laura as Andy fastened him in.

"It's okay, honey. Mommy's here," she said, peeking around Andy, who didn't seem bothered in the least by her son. Gabriel, well, he never looked at Andy, and, thankfully, Andy said nothing as he slid the seat back and Laura climbed in. She reached her hand over the seat, touching her son's shoulder and then his cheek. "It's okay, sweetie."

Gabriel continued to whine, gripping her finger with his tiny little ones. Andy slid in under the wheel, and she didn't miss the way he glanced at Gabriel and then her, as if was trying to figure something out. Laura's face burned bright red. She was so uncomfortable around Andy, and it was because he was so big. His presence, everything about him, took up more space than a person had a right to. Laura was having a hard time breathing.

"Do you want help putting on your seatbelt?" Andy started to reach over, but Laura bumped his hand and fumbled her seatbelt, trying to latch it one handed. She couldn't let go of Gabriel's hand; she worried he'd start screaming and freaking out, and that was about the last thing she wanted Andy to see. Even daycare had been a problem—with how long he had cried, carrying on for hours, no one could console him. It was awful, and Peggy had been furious.

Andy brushed her hand aside and snapped the buckle, pulling it tight. He started the truck and backed out. "Which way?"

Laura pointed, swallowing the lump as his touch, though subtle, burned into her. The worst thing possible was happening, and she could do nothing about it: He was driving her home. "Turn right and then left at the four-way stop."

CHAPTER 3

Andy took his time driving back to the estate. In fact, this was probably the first time he'd ever driven the speed limit and the first time he actually had cars passing him. He needed to think, all because Laura had stumped him. Not many had ever done that. The fact was that Andy read people really well. He'd have to be blind not to pick up on her discomfort and downright embarrassment about everything, from the pathetic daycare that warehoused kids, with that loudmouthed broad who'd done her best to embarrass her, to the fact that she didn't want him to drive her home. It wasn't until he pulled up in front of that rundown home that he'd understood why. Hell, he wouldn't want anyone to know he lived in a dump like that either. A chain-link fence was rusted and falling down in parts, and an overgrown yard looked as if it had never been kept up. A rotted-out sofa sat on the front porch, torn, with the stuffing pulled out.

The scene didn't fit his image of Laura, not that he knew what that was. But then, for a single mother, it had to have been difficult for her to keep up anything. Why wouldn't she live in some apartment? After all, wouldn't that have been easier?

When he parked, she had jumped out quickly, moving the seat forward and lifting her son in her arms before Andy could get around to her side and help her. The boy hadn't talked. He was old enough that Andy wondered why he didn't. He had also whined the entire drive home as if terrified of Andy, and he wouldn't even look Andy's way. Andy wondered if he may have started screaming if he had. Andy didn't know exactly how old Gabriel was, but he didn't miss Laura's worried glances, her flushed face, her acute nervousness. He could even see the beads of sweat dotting her forehead, and he knew she was far from warm. She kept saying over and over, "It's okay. We're almost home. Don't worry, honey."

When Andy came around the truck, she'd shut her door and thanked him for the ride before saying quite sharply, "I'll pay you back for the daycare." Then she'd hurried up the crumbling concrete steps as if she couldn't get away from him fast enough. As Andy climbed behind the wheel, he noticed the way she glanced at the bottom of the front steps and then bit her lower lip, lifting her son. He looked way too heavy for her to be carrying him around, but she scurried around the side of the house as if she didn't want anyone to see her. Andy had sat there for a minute, rubbing his jaw and staring at the dilapidated house, wondering about this big-eyed young lady and what her story was.

He had no intention of accepting one dime from her. The only reason he had paid that loudmouthed busybody was to get her to shut up. He could tell she was just warming up to take a strip off Laura for something that wasn't her fault. Who the hell did she think she was? Andy hadn't missed the way her eyes widened when she saw him with Laura.

He knew the type; Laura's name was as good as mud in the next fifteen minutes. The woman had carried on about money and Laura owing her. Andy thought that just wasn't okay. She should have done it in private, where the entire world couldn't listen in, and that was the only reason he had yanked open his wallet and tossed her five hundred dollars. Laura hadn't deserved to lose her job over a stupid Christmas tree.

What the hell was her story, anyway? Andy slapped the steering wheel. A girl alone with a little boy. He had asked her about family, even a boyfriend. No one. How could she have no one? He didn't miss how pale she'd gotten, and he knew there was more to the story. What he knew was that she was alone with a child who couldn't talk. What he didn't know and planned to find out was where she had come from. Jules would know. Come to think of it, he had no idea how long Laura had worked at the estate.

It didn't take Andy long to track down Jules in the kitchen with the cook, tasting what looked like some kind of sauce the old cook was stirring on the stove. Both women stared at him when he walked in with an odd look that had Andy glancing behind him to see if there was a problem.

"Jules, I need to speak with you." He knew he sounded irritated.

Jules set the spoon on the smooth green counter. The cook was an older, short, plump woman who was still staring at him, holding the wooden spoon in her wrinkled hand. He couldn't remember if he'd ever spoken to her. He blinked as he tried to think of her name, but nothing would come to him.

"Certainly, Mr. Friessen. Would you like to speak with

me in the hallway?" She motioned toward the door and even took a step to leave the kitchen.

"No, here's fine." Andy crossed his arms and didn't miss the way the cook's wrinkled face tightened. She banged a pot with a spoon, making an awful racket, and then yanked open the fridge, pulling out a large pan with a hunk of beef that was marinating and sat it on the counter with a clatter. Andy frowned, not missing the old woman's irritation as her sharp gaze narrowed, and he was positive she was shooting sparks his way.

"Jules, about Laura, the maid, what can you tell me about her?"

Jules had run this household of servants since Andy was a child. She was a large older woman, and her double chin wobbled when she spoke. "Well, not much. She's young. She always came to work, did her job. I'm not sure what it is you'd like to know about her. She's gone. Your mother fired her."

A loud clatter had them both staring at the cook. "Pot slipped," the cook snapped, glaring at Andy with bloodshot eyes that were now shooting shards of ice his way.

Jules' expression became unusually nervous as she glanced at the ceiling and then back at Andy. "Sir, why don't we step out of the kitchen and maybe in the library, where you'd be more comfortable."

"I want to know who hired Laura, how long she's been working here, where she came from." He didn't move but watched the cook this time as he spoke, and she glared right back at him with something that resembled pure venom. For the first time ever, Andy considered taking a step back.

Jules cleared her throat roughly. "Sir, I hired her. She's been here since the spring...."

The old cook snorted, interrupting Jules.

"Aida, enough. Stir your sauce!" Jules shouted at the cook, shoving her hands on her plump hips.

Andy took a step closer to the cook and stopped when she appeared to squeeze the wooden spoon handle in a way that made him think it'd snap in two. The woman had balls, he had to give her that. The way she didn't back down, firming her trembling lips to a fine white line, he was positive that if he stepped any closer, she'd raise her hand and cosh him over the head.

"Aida, is it?" Andy didn't wait for her to respond. "Is there something you want to say?"

"No, sir, she has nothing to say. She has a dinner to prepare, so please, sir, if we could step out..." Jules tried to step in and even extended her hand again toward the door, but Andy cut her off before she could finish.

"No, I want to hear what Aida here has to say."

"You're a pig!" She spat the words at him.

"Oh, Aida!" Jules groaned behind him. "Sir, she didn't mean a word. Please don't fire her. Your mother has five dinner guests arriving this evening, and there is no one to cook dinner if you fire her. Now, Aida, get back to the stove and mind your tongue." Jules clapped her hands.

But Andy was still staring at the tiny old woman, who stared at him as if he were the devil himself, with not a lick of fear anywhere in her. What a tough old broad she was. "Jules, would you shut up? Now, Aida, you're obviously upset with something I've done, so I would like to hear it." Andy glanced sharply at Jules just as she opened her mouth. He was positive she would make another attempt to get him to leave, but he had no intention of walking out that door or anywhere until he heard what this unusual spunky woman had to say. "Jules, I want to hear this. Obviously, there is a problem."

The cook stepped closer to Andy and held up the wooden spoon in front of her face. "You, sir, stay away from that girl. She doesn't need the likes of you making things any more difficult for her. And she's a good girl, she is. She caused no trouble, worked hard, was never late. She asks nothing of no one. She didn't deserve to get fired, and I told Jules just that after I got here and heard what you did. If it wasn't for you and your temper, carrying on like you were, the tree would still be standing now." She waved the spatula in front of his face. "And she will not be your plaything! You stay away from her and her child."

Andy stared at this short old lady, whose face was deeply etched with lines. She didn't cower, look away, or apologize; she stood right in front of him, daring him to step closer, to say something stupid. Frankly, he admired this old woman's gumption, standing up to him, not tiptoeing around him as everyone did.

"I am not interested in making her my plaything...."

The old woman shrieked and cut him off. "Bullshit! Don't think I haven't seen both you and your dad eyeing up that poor girl every time she bent over, knelt down, as if you were imagining all kinds of lewd things to do to her, and with your dad's reputation with bedding women, and yours not much better. Stay away from her."

For the first time in his life, he was speechless. He'd never been spoken to quite like this, and never by an employee. He opened his mouth to say something, but she started shouting again.

"I brought the girl here. She has more hard-working gumption in her little finger than you, and she struggles to give that little boy everything. How is she supposed to feed her child and keep a roof over her head now?" The cook tossed the wooden spoon on the counter, where it clanged against the pot, and untied her apron before yanking off her hairnet and tossing it onto the roast on the counter. She slung her apron over her head and tossed it to Andy, who caught it and looked at it, wondering what the hell had just happened.

"Aida, where are you going?" Jules asked as the cook brushed past her, yanking open a cupboard door and pulling out her purse and coat.

"I quit," Aida snapped.

"Mr. Friessen, stop her. Your mother has guests arriving in two hours, and I'll not be the one telling her the cook quit!" Jules was wringing her hands frantically.

"Aida, wait." Andy handed Jules the white apron and followed the cook out the back door. She strode with her head high around the puddles that had turned everything to mud toward the stables, where the staff parked their cars out of sight. She ignored Andy, but should that really have surprised him? No one had ever ignored him, and Aida marched on faster, as if she was saying, "Good riddance!" Andy had to step it up to catch up to her, as her speed surprised him.

Finally, he jogged up beside her. "Aida, please..."

"You ever stop to think of the repercussions before you do something, Andy Friessen? Your father doesn't." Aida didn't seem to care who heard her as she raked him over the coals.

Several of the hired hands lingering outside turned their heads as Aida's loud voice carried. He couldn't believe the woman had the gall to talk down to him like this.

"Aida, please stop. You're right." For some reason Andy couldn't explain, he didn't want this old woman to hate him, and when she stared at him with bloodshot brown eyes, hatred was exactly what he saw. "Don't quit. The reason I came back to talk to Jules about Laura is because I picked her up on the side of the road while she was walking, and I drove her and her son home to some piece-of-crap house." Andy gestured with his hands and then dropped them, letting out a heavy sigh. My God, he'd never had to work so hard with someone in his life, with someone who worked for him. Humility was a bitter pill to swallow, and this old woman whose head barely reached the top of his chest had taken all of it and slapped it in his face. "She didn't deserve to get fired, and I told my mother that."

Aida finally stopped walking and faced Andy, clutching her purse and coat to her chest as if someone would yank them away. She stared up at Andy, and he looked down on her, someone he could take out in a minute, which was why he couldn't figure out how she put the fear of God into him.

"Laura should have her job back. Get it for her, and I'll come back." She said it so quietly, but the effect hit much like a wrecking ball taking out an old concrete building.

Andy shook his head. "No." He let out a sharp breath. "I'll find her another job, somewhere else. She shouldn't work for my mother. She's not a nice woman."

Aida straightened a little and glared at him. "And where would she find this other job? On her back?"

"No. I'll find her a decent job in town. I don't know where yet, but I will, I promise. Just please stay."

"And you'll stay away from her?" Aida asked.

"I am not my father, and I already told you I wouldn't mistreat Laura. She didn't deserve what happened this morning." Andy knew he hadn't answered her question, and by the way she watched him and then ran her sharp gaze down his chest and back up to his face, he knew she was deciding.

"Fine. By the end of the day, you have a job for her." The cook stalked back toward the house. "And don't think I don't know you didn't agree to stay away from Laura. But heed me: If I hear you're trying to play with that girl, I will call you out." She didn't look back as she spoke.

"Aida," Andy said. She stopped and glanced over her shoulder. "Thank you."

She grunted and stomped back into the house, slamming the door behind her.

CHAPTER 4

ndy couldn't believe he was at the small local airport, a sterile building that catered to the wealthy, with small planes, charters, and private jets, to pick up Alexis, a woman he'd never met and didn't have the slightest interest in getting to know better. He had things on his mind, and he was annoyed about everything here, from the airline clerks behind the counters to the swarm of people trickling steadily in and out of the small building. Even the cheap vinyl seats were an irritation, because he'd had to wait almost half an hour.

Andy knew he could have said no when his mother cornered him again in his library after he'd spoken with Aida. He even contemplated not showing up, but that was not only poor manners but poor business, which was something Andy didn't do, especially when he'd already agreed.

Andy didn't much like the senator, and he definitely wasn't in the mood to spend any time with a spoiled rich girl. He shook his head as he glared out the glass, watching the planes take off and land. He wasn't a man who could be guided around by his nose hairs, which was exactly what his mother was doing by having him pick up Alexis. It was why he was standing here now, staring out this glaring window that showed the fingerprints of every two-year-old who had touched it.

Under normal circumstances, Andy would have no problem not picking up this rich, prissy thing, and he certainly wouldn't be bothered at all by what anyone thought. The only reason he was here now was because of Jed.

He loved his cousin. He'd come a long way in repairing the closeness of their relationship. Growing up, they had been inseparable, even when Jed had moved out here and bought that run-down acreage at a dusty auction on a whim one day. But when Diana came back and Jed married her, well, things were never the same between them. They were like two rutting bulls marking their territory, ripping up the ground, ready to rip each other apart, until the spring, when Jed had set out on the new chestnut stallion he'd got at auction for next to nothing. He had been training him, an unruly beast, to be his lead horse when he took riders out on the trails for pack trips. What Jed had been thinking, Andy still didn't know. Andy shook his head as he remembered staring that stallion in the eye and taking a step back. But Jed loved a challenge, and that stallion had been nothing but. Red, the stallion, had thrown Jed past the open meadow where the trees just began to thicken, and it had been well past dark when he and a very pregnant Diana found Jed leaning against an old fir tree with a broken leg and cracked ribs. That night had brought them closer, helping to heal the hurt between them that had been caused by what he'd done to Diana as a child. It was his shame, not hers, and she was the one woman he would go to his grave loving, a woman who'd never be his.

Jed was the only Friessen to carve out something from that dustbowl piece of land for himself. He wouldn't take a red cent from his daddy. Both he and Diana had worked damn hard to turn his unsuccessful horse-riding outfit into something with a reasonable income. Hell, Andy knew they struggled to get by, but they were happy, and by the way they looked at each other, loved each other, deep down he really tried to be happy for them.

But now, for whatever reason she had in that sharp, calculating mind of hers, his own mother was cozying up to Senator Johnston. He could still feel the ice shards ripping through his veins when he realized she knew about Jed and Diana's expansion to therapeutic riding for disabled kids, and about the funding they had approached the state for. His alarm bells were shrieking.

He had to be careful with Caroline. Even though that sultry, stunning woman who could hold her own in any arena was his mother, he'd learned the hard way over many tears as a kid to be careful with her, making sure that she never knew his weakness. She was sly, much like the coyote, a trickster, with all the added characteristics of a black widow lying silently in her thick, silky web, just waiting for the right moment. It would be over quickly: The bite would be subtle, but a painful poison would quickly spread through him, burning his veins as it ripped apart his every sense of peace. Andy had sworn he'd never fall victim to her schemes, but here he stood in Paine Field, the small airport in Snohomish county, pacing the tiled floor, waiting for Alexis to disembark the private jet that was now taxiing down the runway toward the terminal, lights flashing.

Stairs were wheeled over, and the door popped open. A tall, leggy brunette dressed in dark pants, heeled boots, and a white fur coat climbed down and strode toward the terminal. She walked with confidence as workers scurried around her. The glass door was opened by a security guard. The brunette had long, wavy hair, and she stopped just inside the terminal. One of the workers had to step around her. She didn't appear worried, but she seemed to take in everything as she swept her gaze around the terminal until she locked eyes with Andy. He, of course, could have made it easier and stepped toward her, but he was still pissed at being forced to be here, so his first impression of this chit was one of irritation. She may have been a nice enough girl or a snob, but even though she was quite lovely, he wasn't interested in stoking her fire and definitely wasn't interested in getting to know any part of the lovely body that he was positive was hidden under that expensive fur coat.

The woman didn't smile. What she did do was stride straight toward him, her head high and her shoulders back, clutching a leather purse to her side. She had the confidence in her steps of a woman who knew exactly what she wanted.

"You must be Andy Friessen." She stuck out her hand and stared at him with icy blue eyes.

"I am indeed. You must be Alexis Johnston." He accepted her soft hand, a strong, firm handshake.

She smiled, flashing brilliant, straight white teeth. She reminded him so much of the women he'd dated in the past, but it had been a long while since he'd dated anyone, and she did nothing to entice him, even though she was extremely attractive.

"You have bags?" Andy asked, just as a man in black pants and a dusty blue sports coat pushed a squeaky cart with three large red suitcases toward him.

"Ma'am, where would you like me to put your bags?"

the young employee asked Alexis before glancing Andy's way.

"My truck's this way." Andy gestured toward the door and started walking, only stopping to glance over his shoulder when he realized Alexis wasn't beside him or even following. She had a set of full red lips that at one time he'd have found a way to sample, even with the frown she'd pasted on now. "Is there a problem?" Andy gestured impatiently and waited while she let out a huff and then strode toward him and past him.

Why, he'd pissed her off! She must have expected him to give her his arm, but he wasn't interested. She was one foxy lady, with that oval face, round cheeks, strong chin. From her open coat, he could tell she was slim and curvy. In her heels, she was the perfect height. Her head topped his shoulders, but there was something cold as ice about her, so reserved that he could feel her coil up and pull away, and it chilled him to the bone.

"The blue truck. Just toss the bags in back," Andy said to the employee, who did just that, lifting the bags and tossing them into the back of the truck.

"Be careful with that," Alexis said. "What's in there is worth more than you'll have in a lifetime." She set her hands on her shapely hips. The tips of her red fingernails really stood out against the backdrop of the black silky blouse she'd exposed when she brushed open her coat. By her blue eyes, which were outlined in mascara and light brown shadow, Andy had no doubt she was a cold bitch, too. Andy glanced upward and then shook his head in sympathy at the young guy, who was looking to Andy for help as he held the last suitcase, then shrugged and tossed it in, too.

"Thanks," Andy said, but then the guy just stood

looking at Andy, not Alexis, and Andy didn't miss the way Alexis tapped her toe and stared at him, raising one eyebrow. "Unbelievable," he said as he reached into his jean pocket and pulled out his wallet, handing ten dollars to the airport employee. "Wait," he said as he handed him another twenty. "For your trouble." Andy glanced at Alexis when he said it.

"Thank you, sir." The man actually smirked before he hurried back into the airport.

Andy started walking around the side of his truck. He didn't have to turn and look to know Alexis was waiting for him to open her door, but he'd be damned if he was having any of that. He knew he was being a prick, but he hoped she got the message loud and clear. Evidently not, as she was still standing on the curb when he slid behind the wheel.

"Oh, for the love of God," he muttered under his breath. He climbed out and strode around to the passenger door, yanking the damn thing open.

"Well, thank you. I was starting to wonder if all forms of courtesy were void in this part of the country." As soon as she slid onto the leather seat, he shoved the door closed and smiled as he listened to the slam and her squeak of outrage.

CHAPTER 5

"Your rent is due on the first of the month. There are no exceptions."

Laura stood in the open doorway, facing her landlord, Jerry Hines, a middle-aged single guy with a solid build. He was tall and a little on the rough side at times, which made him somewhat good looking, but he could be a hard nose. He'd raised her rent only once, and she knew it was more than he was legally allowed, but there wasn't much she could do about it. She knew if she complained too hard or at all she'd find herself tossed onto the street on her ass, and no one would step in and help her.

"I know, Mister Hines. I am a few days late, but I lost my job, and my boss didn't give me my last paycheck. I'm looking for another one. If you could just give me a few more days..."

He cut her off. " No, cash now. Do you or don't you have it?" he stated in a harsh, deep tone that sent a shiver crawling up her back.

A hard lump burned her throat, and she swallowed hard, trying to dislodge it, and scrambled for anything, hoping for a miracle. She had not a clue what to do, and she shut her eyes for a second and pressed her fingertips to her closed lids. That was when she felt his touch as he leaned in and fingered a strand of her long hair, which draped over her shoulder. Her eyes popped open, and she dropped her hands and watched as he slid his hand on the doorframe in a gesture that had her blood running cold.

"There is another way you could work it off for this month." He gazed at her with dark eyes that resembled those of a predator cornering his prey. She could almost see something slithering, something speckled and ugly, and for a moment it seeped into her, cutting her skin. Laura stepped back, trembling, because she'd never experienced this from a man before, and it terrified the hell out of her.

"No. Please, I would like just a couple days, and I swear I will have your rent. I could give you my car." She felt panic, a strange bedfellow that had become too familiar over the last few years, sneaking up again and squeezing her lungs until she found it a struggle to breathe. Her heart was pounding so hard she wondered if he could hear it, because she could feel the beat pounding right down to her bare toes in a pair of worn-out slippers.

Jerry sighed, and his expression hardened into something that was now unreachable. The interest that had flared for her in his eyes just moments ago disappeared into a hard wall as he watched her as if she were nothing but a nuisance. "That piece of crap? Not interested. I want you gone by morning. I have someone who'll be moving in."

"Jerry, please... We have no place to go. Don't we have any rights? How can you just throw us out? I've always paid you on time. This is the first time ever..." She didn't recognize her voice as it cracked and trembled. The edge of panic was all around her now, biting her ass and tossing her into a black hole of nothing. The unknown was too much; the fear wouldn't even register.

He turned away and then shook his head, just watching her with those hard eyes as if saying, "You had your chance and you blew it." Then he leaned in as if to bite her and said in a voice laced with venom, "You have no rights. You're a nobody, and I have the law on my side. I'm a landowner. Laura, you're a nice girl, but don't mess with me, because you'll get hurt. Start packing. I'll be back at seven in the morning, and you better be gone or I will take what you owe me in another way, and then I'll toss you in the street." He didn't stop but took the stairs up two at a time and disappeared around the corner.

Laura closed the door with the loose doorknob and sagged against it as if she were an eighty-year-old woman. She couldn't believe what was being thrown at her. She'd been struggling for so long to keep her head above water, but she could feel herself drowning as her lungs burned and she gasped for breath. What had she done to deserve this? It was one cruel thing after another, as if she were freefalling into all this unjustness and darkness, with every bad thing slamming into her over and over. She had no family she could pick up the phone and call, not that she had a phone anyway, though she'd happily walk to the gas station and use the grubby pay phone outside, but she couldn't, because her parents had tossed her out when she'd stood before them at fifteen, trembling, and confessing to them that she was four months pregnant. Her mother had kept asking why she was gaining weight, and she couldn't hide it and knew it would be bad when they found out. But when her mother called her a slut and her father turned away from her, she'd felt the floor shatter beneath her. Her mother had done all the yelling and screaming and then accused her of being a bad influence on her younger brothers.

She'd been only fifteen when she was handed a suitcase and told to leave, so she'd worked part time at a fast food restaurant until she gave birth to Gabriel a few months after her sixteenth birthday.

Tyler, the sixteen-year-old boy who'd gotten her pregnant, refused to have anything to do with her. She'd gone to him after her parents threw her out, but he'd shut the door in her face and said, "Leave me alone," so after Gabriel was born, she'd called her mom, believing that time and distance had softened her. But she'd outright refused to come see the baby, saying that she and Laura's father would allow her to come home only if she gave the baby away. Standing in that sterile hospital hallway, barefoot in her hospital gown, holding the payphone, she'd stared at the receiver feeling as though her mother had just reached through and sliced her stomach open with a knife. After fifteen hours of labor, emotionally battered beyond anything she'd experienced before, she'd burst into tears and slowly hung up the phone. Shortly after, with her baby Gabriel, she'd snuck out of the hospital and left Arlington, and she hadn't looked back.

Now, four years later, they lived hand to mouth. She needed the paycheck that Mrs. Friessen refused to give her to pay this month's rent and buy food for her and Gabriel. Laura gazed at the one-room basement suite with the sagging double bed in the corner, a dated worn beige sofa, a small kitchen table with two chairs, a cooktop stove, and a camper fridge that was cracked along the top.

Laura strode to the beige tweed sofa, which had a spring poking up from the middle cushion. This and all the furniture here belonged to Jerry. Laura dropped down before her knees gave out on her and watched Gabriel, her dark-haired little boy, playing with the wooden blocks she'd picked up at the second-hand store. He was oblivious to anything going on around him and unaware someone had just been there.

"Hey, buddy, we're going to go for a car ride in a bit."

She slid off the sofa onto the floor and snagged her jeans on something sharp. The pain that jabbed her skin right then was welcome but did little to distract her from the agony of what she had to do. She glanced around at their meager possessions. She didn't have much: A few dishes, two pots, a box that held their clothes, the blankets, everything would most likely fit in the trunk of her car.

She didn't know how long she sat on the dirty carpeted floor, but she knew it was getting late, and she dared not be there when Jerry came back. She was still shaking from his threat and what she saw in his eyes. She was scared of what he'd do to her, and with her son watching.

It took her about a dozen trips to pack up her blankets, her clothes, Gabriel's toys, and the small amount of food she had. The fridge was mostly bare except for milk and cheese, but it was cold enough outside that the food wouldn't go bad in the trunk.

Just as the sun settled on the edge of the horizon and the first raindrops splattered on the ground, in the grass, creating puddles everywhere, Laura Parnell started her car and pulled away from her rundown rented suite in the rusted-out Volvo that squeaked as she cranked the wheel and rattled when she pressed the gas, a car she'd picked up for two hundred dollars just last year.

CHAPTER 6

"Couldn't you at least have put on a suit and tie?" Caroline whispered before turning and pasting a graceful smile on her face when Alexis walked into Andy's library wearing a short black dress with a scoop neckline that outlined her curvaceous figure and pumps that showed off her sexy, long slim legs. Her dark, rich hair had been curled and hung in thick waves, her makeup was impeccable, and she carried herself as Andy imagined any politician's daughter would.

Andy shot his mother a glare he hoped would scorch just a bit, and maybe she'd back off. But no, not Caroline. He should have known better, so he stalked over to the bar and lifted a crystal decanter, pouring himself a generous amount of bourbon. Caroline had called him out: He had made no effort to clean up, wearing his dark jeans and red shirt with the top two buttons open. In fact, he hadn't even shaved again today, and he always made a point of shaving before dinner, especially when there were guests. His father, Todd, whistled as he strolled in, obviously following orders, as he was dressed in a dark suit and blue silk tie.

"Alexis, you look absolutely stunning." Todd stopped beside Alexis and leaned down and kissed her on the cheek, then strode to Caroline and kissed the cheek she offered. He played his part well, and Andy almost raised his glass in a salute to good old Dad before swallowing a mouthful of bourbon.

Andy leaned against the bar, watching his mother. She was a damn fine actress, and she flipped a switch when important guests were present, as if she were the loving wife and Todd the devoted husband. The two of them could have won an award with their performance, but then, there were so many sides to each of them. Someone with a split personality, who flip-flopped back and forth in persona like a swinging pendulum, would have nothing on the two of them. Tonight he was watching the art of politics at work. He wondered to himself if there was in fact a course that couples took before stepping into the political arena, teaching a wife how to smile, hug, and kiss her husband in public when she'd rather claw his eyes out.

Alexis didn't seem bothered in the least by Caroline and Todd's performance, but then, she was a senator's daughter, so this would seem normal. She stepped around the leather sofa in front of the fireplace and sat, sliding one slim leg outlined in silky sheer stockings over the other. Caroline took Andy's usual wing chair and slid back, crossing her legs.

"Oh, Andy, pour me a glass of wine, please. Alexis, would you like a glass of wine?" Caroline gestured with her hand, showing off her freshly manicured nails.

"Yes, that would be lovely. Red, if you have it?" She didn't smile at Andy. Instead, she glanced around the room, looking anywhere except at him.

"Alexis, we are so glad you're here as our guest. I was

just telling your father this afternoon when I spoke with him how much we were looking forward to this visit."

Andy turned his back and poured the two glasses of wine. He handed one to his mother and the other to Alexis.

"Thank you, Andy," said Alexis.

If anything, she had impeccable manners. She glanced his way and gave him an artificial smile that had none of the light he'd seen flashing there earlier.

"Andy, Alexis is going to be here for the next few weeks. Apparently, she's quite the horse person, and it would be lovely if you could take her out for a ride. Take her on the miles of trails behind our property, the ones you're always bragging about." Caroline swept her hand elegantly. "Andy, sit down and join us."

Of course, where she was pointing was right beside Alexis, and although Andy had no problem flexing his muscles and being rude at times, and a real prick at others, this time his conscience wouldn't let him. He joined Alexis on the sofa and caught the gleam in his dad's eye right before he took a swig of the scotch he'd just poured for himself. So he, too, was in on it. Talk about selling him out —his dad had never pulled this on him before.

"Alexis, I haven't been out riding in a while, but I don't mind taking you out. We also have a riding ring that you're more than welcome to make use of. I'll let Ben, our stable manager, know. He can get you matched up with a horse."

Todd crossed his booted foot over his knee, showing off his alligator skin boots, and interrupted Andy. "Oh, Andy, as Alexis is our guest, why don't you look after that? Ben is far too busy, and, Alexis, I think you might be more comfortable with Andy. He really is a master with horses. Come on, Andy, I know you can take one look at this lovely lady beside you and know the perfect horse for her." His father then raised his eyebrows as if he should know better than to argue.

"Why, I would love to spend some time riding. That's if you have time, Andy? After all, your mother has invited me to stay through the New Year, and I would love it if you could show me the trails and the horses." She held up her glass and slid around until her leg bumped Andy. Andy gritted his teeth until he felt something in his jaw pop.

"Dinner is ready," Jules announced.

Andy jumped up and sloshed his drink on his jeans.

His mother frowned. "Come, Alexis. Let's head into the dining room. Andy will join us after he's changed." The women left the library chatting about this and that, but Todd grabbed Andy's arm before he stepped out of the room.

"What's the matter with you? This is the senator's daughter. Be a little more friendly, it shouldn't be difficult. She's not that hard on the eyes," Todd growled in a low voice as he leaned in.

Andy had never seen irritation quite like this in his father's eyes. "I'm not interested, and what the hell is Mother doing, inviting her to stay past New Year's? I'll be bumping into her every time I turn around. I'm not interested in either of you stepping into my personal life and pushing any woman in my direction. You should know better, Dad, so just back off." Andy was irritated. He'd been distracted lately, but tonight he hadn't missed how both Todd and Caroline were pushing Alexis in his path. Just what the hell was going on?

"Look, son. I happen to agree with your mother on this one. She's a fine catch. Get to know her. Spend some time with her. Woo her. She's probably great in bed. But this is an alliance I want, that your mother wants. There are benefits for us. You don't need to fall in love with the girl, but I do want you married by spring and to have her pregnant by the fall." Todd set his glass on the bar and squeezed Andy's shoulder. "Listen, son, it's time you settled down, anyway. Have some kids. Give us some grandkids. It'll look good. It's time you do your part for this family."

Andy stared at Todd as if he'd lost his mind. "I don't give a shit about an alliance. No one pushes any woman on me, ever. When I marry a woman, it will be a woman I'm in love with, not because of political clout or money. That's your game, Dad, not mine." Andy knocked back the rest of his drink and then set his glass down on the side of the bar, but the smile dancing in Todd's eyes pushed all his buttons. He started to leave but hesitated when Todd chuckled.

"Son, you have no idea what's in store for you. If you don't make this happen, your cousin Jed and that Claremont piece of trash he married will lose their ranch. You may not be happy about what you need to do, but you will do it, and I know that by next year, you'll be thanking me," Todd said matter-of-factly.

Andy slid his gaze over his father, watching the man for the first time as if he didn't know who he was. Maybe he hadn't heard him right, but as he stared and watched the sly grin move across a face that was so similar to his own but twenty years older, with graying hair and cool, icy eyes staring back at him, it was then that the truth sank in. His father and mother had formed some alliance, and he was the pawn. He felt as if his feet were surrounded in cement blocks, as he couldn't move and take one step out of that room. He realized the bastard had told Caroline of Andy's one weakness, his love for Jed. Any threat to Jed would bring Andy to heel, but this made absolutely no sense. Andy and his dad loved each other; Andy had cleaned up everything for years after his dad, every screw up, every trail of broken hearts he'd left strewn from one side of the road to the other, one woman after another, so what was really going on that would have Todd selling his son down the river?

"Why would you do this to your own nephew?" Andy asked. He needed to know because if Todd did this to Jed, Andy knew without a doubt that Jed's father, Rodney Friessen, and brothers, Brad and Neil, would all swoop in and take Todd on, and only a fool would take on Rodney Friessen. Todd was not a stupid man—far from it. So as Andy watched the hardness in his father for the first time, he didn't know what the hell to expect, and that worried him.

Todd never smiled when he said, "This is business, son. Just remember something, too. When Jed took up with that Claremont trash, he spit on his family, on me, so I no longer have his back. Just remember that. When you turn your back on your family, you're dead to them." Todd patted Andy on the shoulder as he brushed past. "Look on the bright side: Alexis is easy on the eyes and could be a whole lot of fun in bed. Love's... got no place in a marriage. That's when a woman has the power to take you down. If you want fun, have it on the side. Hurry up and change. Don't keep the ladies waiting." Todd whistled as he strode arrogantly into the foyer.

Andy glanced at the front door, the brass handle that wasn't far away. He could just walk out the door. As he stepped closer, he had to swallow his anger and clamp his jaw shut when he almost shouted out to his father—and his mother—that they could go to hell. But there was something going on that he didn't like. He could smell the foul stench now, as if something were lying dead in the middle of the floor. As he reached out to grab the handle of the front door, he dropped his hand to his side and turned, taking in the huge grand entry and the black and white marble floor, the grandfather clock, the hall tables, and all the priceless antiques here and there. He listened to the laughter and the voices from Caroline, Todd, and Alexis drifting from the dining room and then hustled upstairs, changing into dark slacks and a clean dress shirt. When he hurried back down, he bumped into the old cook, who had a meanness in her eyes and a hairnet strung over her short, graying hair.

She planted both hands on her ample hips. "Did you find her a job?" she barked.

"Who?" He blinked and wondered at the way her bloodshot eyes flared as if she were going to hit him.

"Laura! You gave me your word." Her voice was getting louder, so Andy rested his hand on her shoulder and gestured toward the library with his other hand.

"Let's go in the library."

Aida stopped just inside the library and knocked his hand away.

"Look I'm sorry. Something came up, but I will first thing in the morning. I'll make sure she's taken care of. I promise."

The cook glared at him again. "You make sure it's first thing, or find yourself another cook." She stalked away.

Andy smacked his forehead with the edge of his fist. How could he have forgotten about Laura and her little boy and the dump they lived in? *Come on, Andy, pull it together.* He'd planned to make some calls, tossing around a few ideas, but when he had stepped out of his truck to make those calls, his foreman had shouted from the open barn door where he stood with the vet. One of the mares was foaling, and there were complications. An eight year old Roan, Trudy Bell, was having her first foal, and it had been after midnight when the vet pulled the hind legs out and the foal came out backwards. Andy had helped to hold the mare down, and it was three in the morning when he had finally gone to bed.

"Dammit, Andy," he bit out in irritation as he jammed his fingers thought his short, neatly clipped hair. He let out a low growl as he didn't like this feeling of being pulled in two different directions. After dinner, he'd excuse himself and then go make some calls, find Laura a job and a decent place to live. Perfect. He could see the checkmark already marking off this task, one less thing on his plate. Then he would find out what his parents were up to and why there was a sudden urgency to have him married to a rich, foxy lady.

CHAPTER 7

Andy knocked on the wooden screen door of the run-down house where Laura Parnell lived. He listened to the creak of the floor as someone approached and the inside door swung open, and an extremely overweight woman with gray hair and a cigarette dangling from her lips stared up at him.

"Yeah?" was all she said through the closed screen door. Smoke drifted up into his face.

Andy coughed and waved the smoke away. "I'm looking for Laura. Is she home?"

The woman scratched her head with her stubby, wrinkled fingers. Her short gray hair was an untidy mess. "Who?" She truly looked confused, and then she pulled the cigarette from her lips and coughed a deep smoker's cough until tears shimmered in her eyes.

"Laura Parnell, young, blonde, good-looking girl. She's got a little boy. I dropped her off here a few days ago. She lives here." Andy was pointing to the spot he was standing, and he wanted to shake the old lady when she nodded as if having to think about it.

"Oh, yeah, the one with the kid who lived in the basement suite." The woman choked and coughed again.

"Lived? What do you mean 'lived'? They're still there, aren't they?"

The woman shook her head. "Sorry, sonny. Jerry, owns this dump and a few of the other houses on this block." She pushed open the screen door and gestured with the cigarette in her hand to the older run-down homes on the street. "He tossed her out yesterday. She couldn't pay the rent. Saw her load up what she could in that old car last night, and I haven't seen her since." She stepped back inside, and Andy sniffed the off odor coming from the house. It was beyond cigarettes, and he didn't have to look too hard to see the clutter stacked and piled here and there. He was wondering whether she had garbage everywhere when she started to close the door.

Andy pressed his hand there, holding it open. "How do you get to the basement suite?"

"Back of the house. But, sonny, I'm telling you she's gone. You don't mess with Jerry. He wants you out, you're out." This time, she shut the door, and Andy heard the lock click.

He glanced at the rotted-out sofa sitting on the porch beside the door and the boxes beside it, the black bags that he was sure were filled with garbage. He shook his head as he strode down the rotted, creaking steps and around the house to a very different backyard, which was neat and tidy. He paused for a moment, taking in the difference from the front. Andy was surprised and kept going to a set of concrete steps that led down to an open door. He strode down the steep steps, no railing, and listened to a banging and scraping coming from inside. "Laura?" Andy called out as he tapped on the open door and stepped inside. He heard something clatter again, and then a guy shouted, "She's gone."

Andy took in the narrow hallway, sagging yellow roof, stained walls and mold growing from spots along the floor. He stepped around the corner, glancing at a solidly built guy with a wrench fixing a tap. "Where did she go?"

The guy dropped the wrench, gazed at Andy, and smirked. "Who knows? Told her to clear out of here. She couldn't pay the rent."

Andy rested his hand on the faded yellow cracked counter, fighting the urge to deck this prick. "You just threw a single mom with a kid out into the cold?" He had to bite his tongue when the irony hit him. Hadn't he done the same thing fifteen years ago to Diana, Jed's wife, when she was just a kid? Maybe that was what he recognized in this prick before him. It was a darkness he'd come to realize lurked in everyone, a predator, and it was something that men recognized in other men, especially when they had done things to women that they weren't proud of. Maybe that was why Andy wanted to ram his fist down this vile piece of crap's throat. But he didn't. Instead, he flexed his fist.

"Any idea where she went?" Andy glanced around at the torn tweed sofa, which belonged in a dumpster, a lumpy bed in the corner, and a badly stained carpet, all of which had him wondering how someone could live in a dump like this. For the love of God, it was a wonder Laura and her kid weren't sick.

"No, and don't care. Anything else? Because I need to get this place ready for new tenants moving in today." The guy sounded irritated, as if he'd been wronged in some way.

Maybe it was curiosity that had him asking, "What would you charge for a place like this?"

"Eight hundred." The guy swore as he broke off the rusted tap.

Andy glanced around again, because he wouldn't have let a dog stay in this hellhole. "That's highway robbery."

"Yeah, well, finding places to rent ain't easy, so if you want a roof over your head, you have to pay for it. After all, I'm providing a service to all those who need a home."

Andy watched as the guy replaced the tap with something that didn't look much better than what had been there before. "What's your name?"

The big guy stopped what he was doing and looked at Andy. "Jerry Hines."

"Well, Jerry, if you hear from Laura, you tell her I'm looking for her and to call me." Andy pulled a card from his wallet and dumped it on the chipped counter.

Jerry glanced at the card and then flushed. Andy turned and left, feeling nausea squeeze the edge of his stomach. He took the stairs two at a time as he heard the man shout after him, "You can bet, Mister Friessen, if I hear from her, I'll make sure she calls you."

CHAPTER 8

Laura glanced around the dumpster and then stepped closer to the gas station bathroom. She peeked the other way before opening the door. Gabriel stood behind her quietly, holding her hand. She had used the dirty sink to clean them up as best she could. Tucking a cloth, a towel, and a bar of soap in the plastic bag she carried, she then returned the key to the balding, overweight attendant behind the counter.

Her neck ached from sleeping, or trying to sleep, in the torn vinyl passenger seat. She'd made a bed for Gabriel on the backseat so he'd be able to stretch out. She'd parked behind the gas station last night and was pretty sure no one had seen her. She didn't have much gas, so she couldn't afford to be driving all over town. She only had $24.37 left in cash after she'd emptied the pennies from the cigarette tray. Her stomach rumbled as she sat Gabriel in the backseat. She opened the trunk and pulled out a loaf of bread and a jar of peanut butter that was almost empty. She scraped what was left in the jar with one of two plastic knifes she had and spread it on a piece of bread.

There was a lot to plan, to organize, just to survive outside. She glanced at the square concrete building of the gas station and the door that swung open from the bathroom. Another patron leaving. She wouldn't be able to keep using the same bathroom; she'd have to wait for shift change. The guy behind the counter was already giving her odd looks that had her heart pounding her hands sweating. No, she'd have to figure out where another bathroom was for them to use, and then maybe another when it was dark so they could wash up again.

Laura had considered driving to Marysville, but she didn't think her car would make it, the way it backfired and jerked each time she started it now. Anyhow, she didn't have enough gas to make it that far, so it was a moot point. A larger city center would mean more jobs, places to live, maybe a soup kitchen to feed her and Gabriel until they could get back on their feet and she could earn a paycheck. She didn't know who to ask, who to talk to, but she needed to find some answers quickly.

Laura rummaged in her trunk and pulled out a blue knitted hat from a bag of clothes and stuck it onto Gabriel's head as he chewed and swallowed his peanut butter sandwich. Laura rummaged through the plastic bag of food and counted. There were only two slices of bread left, a half box of crackers, two apples, two cans of soup—which she couldn't open, anyway. Gabriel had finished off the cereal yesterday and the milk the night before. The paycheck she should have gotten two days ago would have paid the rent and bought some food. She squeezed her eyes shut as her stomach ached even more. She couldn't get that damn paycheck out of her mind. She was owed that money. She needed it, she deserved it, but there was no way in hell Caroline Friessen was going to give it to her and there was nothing Laura could do about it.

She didn't make much as a maid, but it was enough to get by. She'd managed when the rent was only five hundred dollars, but when Jerry jacked up the rent for that damp, musty suite to eight hundred, it had become really tight, and she'd lain awake several nights worrying and trying to figure out how she'd pay for everything. Then she'd grabbed a local paper and started searching for another place to live, but there weren't too many landlords wanting to rent to single moms and nothing in the price range she needed. So she had cut what she could from their food budget and had stopped driving, catching a ride to the Friessen estate with another maid or anyone who was going to work the same time as her. Daycare, even with the subsidy, took up what was left. It was damn impossible to put any money away.

After Gabriel swallowed his food, Laura wiped his hands with one of the cloths she'd dampened in the dirty gas station bathroom. She had to swallow the saliva that was watering in her mouth from the peanut butter she wiped from Gabriel's fingers, because she was hungry, starving, actually. Her stomach had been rumbling since last night, but until she lined up some kind of job today, she couldn't take food from her son. "Come on, honey. Let's go for a walk."

Laura led her son down the sidewalk of downtown North Lakewood, past the vacant storefronts with rental signs stuck in most of the dirty glass windows. She glanced in at the shops that were still in business but hadn't yet opened for the day. She wondered if any of them would give her work. She hoped so, even though not one had a help wanted sign in the window. She stopped in front of the small grocery store; a young lady with hair tied back in a ponytail flipped the open sign around. Laura pushed open the door.

"Excuse me," she said to the clerk wearing the orange and white uniform shirt. "I was wondering if you could tell me if you're hiring for any job at all?"

The girl frowned as she ran her gaze over Laura and then shook her head. "I don't think so, but you can check with Mister Harris. He's in the back." She pointed to the rear of the store.

"Thank you," Laura said gratefully. She kept Gabriel's hand tucked safely in hers and walked to the double doors that led into the back. She froze, because the sign said "Employees only." For the life of her, she didn't know what to do. Should she knock or just push it open? Thank heavens, she was saved from complete embarrassment when the doors were pushed open by an older man with round, ruddy cheeks, who was pulling a cart loaded with produce boxes.

"Excuse me, I'm looking for Mister Harris." Laura cleared her throat when her voice shook. Gabriel started whining and pulling on her hand. Her face burned crimson. "Gabriel, please let Mommy talk."

The older man glanced at Gabriel, and she could feel his irritation when her son wouldn't stop whining. "I'm Mister Harris."

"I'm so sorry. He's tired. I'm looking for a job and was wondering if you're hiring?"

Gabriel wouldn't stand still, which was so unlike him, and he was trying to pull away now. She had to look away from Mr. Harris, which was extremely rude, but Gabriel was becoming unreasonable. Then she realized he was reaching for the cheese in the cooler beside her. "No, honey, don't touch. I'm sorry—he loves cheese." Laura tried to smile as she jerked her gaze up at the older man frowning at her now. Her smile felt brittle as she gripped Gabriel's hand.

"No, I have nothing available. Sorry, miss." He walked away, pulling the steel cart. Laura felt tears burn the back of her eyes, and her heart sink heavily in her chest. She glanced at the block of orange cheese. Gabriel squealed and then yelled as he reached over for it. Laura just stared at the block of cheese, her mouth watering and her heart sinking again as she stared at the price. It cost over six dollars; she couldn't spare it.

"No, Gabriel."

He wouldn't listen to her, so she lifted him and hurried down the aisle and out the door as he made clicking noises and started whimpering, his hand reaching over her shoulder behind her. Laura didn't stop and look, but she could feel people staring, their eyes and judgement burning into her.

"Miss, wait," a woman's voice called out.

Laura turned and stared at a redheaded young woman who was standing on the sidewalk behind her. Laura's stomach pinched as she clutched Gabriel and lifted him higher so he was propped on her hip. She needed to get out of here so she could calm Gabriel down, but this young, pleasant woman didn't seem annoyed at all. In fact, she strode to Laura, her head high. With a warm smile, she shoved her hands in the front pockets of a plain brown coat. Laura was struck by two things, the warmth that she felt coming from the woman and the fact that she had the most brilliant blue eyes Laura had ever seen.

"I overheard in the store you're looking for a job?" the woman asked, ignoring the way Gabriel was carrying on. It was almost soothing, which took some of the edge off

Laura's stress now pinching every muscle all the way up her spine.

"Yes, I am. I need a job. I'm so sorry, the way he's carrying on. He doesn't always understand...." Laura could hear the panic bite into her voice.

The woman stopped her when she rested a warm hand on Laura's bare one, which was clutching Gabriel and holding him to her. "Don't apologize, please. I was just getting groceries. But I am looking for help. If you're interested, maybe we could go next door to Merle's, have a coffee. I didn't get a chance to eat, so I'd love to buy you and your son breakfast, too, if you haven't eaten. We could talk about the job. That's if you're interested?" The woman's eyes widened, reflecting deep caring and concern out at Laura.

Laura did everything she could not to cry, and she must have looked like a shrew as she struggled to hold it in. She nodded because she couldn't get the words out. "Thank you... Yes."

"Let me just run back in before they think I abandoned my groceries. I'll be right back. Please don't go anywhere." She looked concerned, as if Laura would bolt.

"We'll wait." Laura set Gabriel down, who was still fussing, and kneeled as the pretty woman hurried back into the store. "Gabriel, please stop for Mommy. This nice woman is going to buy us breakfast. Pancakes, would you like pancakes? I know how much you love them. Please, Gabriel, be good. Please, be quiet. I really need this job, whatever it is. Please." She pleaded with Gabriel until he quieted down, she was glad and hoped he understood. Laura couldn't always tell, but at least he wasn't carrying on, and she knew food would keep him occupied. He had to be as hungry, even though he had eaten bread with peanut butter. The pancakes were a luxury and something they hadn't had since Jerry jacked up the rent, but she was sure he remembered.

The woman appeared a minute later, dashing toward Laura. "Thank you so much for having breakfast with me. This is my treat. By the way, my name is Diana Friessen."

Laura's hand froze just as Diana touched hers, and it was then she felt a momentary panic.

"Miss?" the woman asked as if sensing her distress, as she tilted her head and looked at Laura kindly.

"Laura, my name's Laura."

"I recognize that look. I had it once, not so long ago." She patted Laura's hand again. "Let's go have breakfast, Laura."

CHAPTER 9

Diana Friessen hurried back to the grocery store where she'd left her groceries. She could have kicked herself for not asking Laura for her phone number or where she lived. She'd arranged to pick Laura and her son up in the morning. Laura insisted on meeting outside the grocery store, which Diana did find odd, but then, she hadn't been able to pull much personal history from the girl. The girl had a wall so thickly built around her that Diana knew it would take a pick and a whole lot of work to find her way in. But then, Diana knew better than anyone, that when trust was burned, it took everything a person had to open her heart and begin trusting again. She sensed that in this young girl.

Diana hadn't been hungry when she'd taken Laura and her unusually quiet son to the restaurant. In fact, she'd just left the ranch and her husband, Jed, with their eight-month-old baby, Danny. They'd shared a breakfast of ham and eggs before she headed to town to get groceries early, arriving before the store opened and being let in by the clerk. When she'd pushed her shopping cart filled with groceries down the dairy aisle, she'd spotted the young mom with a little boy wearing a look of desperation she'd recognized, all because of what she'd lived through as a child, growing up dirt poor. She couldn't help overhearing the young girl pleading with Mr. Harris, the uptight older man who owned this grocery store. He'd been one of many people who'd shunned Diana when she first returned to North Lakewood, all because of who her mother was. The girl needed work, fast. She needed help, and it angered Diana that Mr. Harris could turn his back on that. Diana couldn't do the same, because she recognized the look of hunger, the way they gazed with such deep longing at the food as if there were an imaginary wall that kept them from reaching in and picking it up. It was a deep pain in their expression that only someone who cared or understood what it was like could see. It was the look of someone who had to go without eating because there wasn't enough money to buy food. The way the little boy had reached for the cheese, whining and carrying on, Diana knew. She also knew, while she watched Laura and her son, that there was something about him that wasn't quite right.

She'd been glad when Laura allowed her to buy them breakfast. The girl looked pitiful, her long hair brushed and stuck under an old gray cap. Her worn coat didn't look all that warm, and it took Diana only a second to realize her zipper was broken. When she sat in that booth in the restaurant, holding the menu and glancing awkwardly at the waitress and then Diana, ordering toast and water only but pancakes for her son, Diana had insisted she try the special, a ham and cheese omelette, and the girl nearly wept before agreeing. When Diana asked her how old she was, the girl had blushed and whispered, "Twenty." It only took Diana a moment to realize how bad the situation was.

She was pale, blond, and thin, with enticing blue eyes that should have belonged to someone far older than her twenty years. Her name was Laura Parnell, a single mother. Laura didn't part with much. She held a lot of closely guarded secrets and was wearing them like a shield. Diana had to tread carefully, because the last thing she wanted to do was spook her and have her grab her little boy and run. She could see something there just below the surface that was so raw.

When Diana asked her if she knew other Friessens, because she had been visibly bothered when Diana said her name, Laura had blushed furiously and lowered her eyes, saying she'd worked at the Friessen mansion and had been fired by his Mrs. Friessen a few days earlier.

What in the world was she going to have the girl do? Diana worried what Jed would say. The thing was she couldn't turn her back on this girl and her son. They just needed someone to care enough to help them. She told Laura, who shoveled the eggs in her mouth so fast that Diana knew it may have been a while since her last meal, about the therapeutic riding she and Jed were starting for children with special needs. It was a dream of hers to help these kids, because there was something special and magical that happened when a child connected with a horse. Diana mentioned to her that maybe her son could be part of it while she was working for her and her husband at the ranch. She was creating the job on the fly and hoped the girl was picking up on the fact that Diana didn't have any idea what she could do. She mentioned the phone; she needed someone to answer it, and there was also so much paperwork when they first started out, just to get their business off the ground.

Diana had to fight the urge to reach across the table and

grab this girl's hand. To tell her it was going to be okay. She could feel, she could smell and see the desperation that she herself had lived through, so her conscience wouldn't let her walk away. She remembered all too well the pain and hurt of praying every single day for just one person to care, to reach out their hand and help. And Diana intended to do just that.

She parked Jed's truck beside her silver SUV in front of their older home, which Jed was slowly renovating with a recent addition he'd framed in but hadn't started building yet for all the kids he hoped they'd have.

"What'd you do, drive to Marysville?" Jed scowled as he strode out of the house, carrying Danny, who grinned and cooed at his mother.

"No, but I did hire a young girl to come and work for us."

Jed stared at Diana in that hard way of his and handed her their baby. "He's hungry and doesn't like the bottle. He wants the real thing." Jed lifted two paper bags of groceries from the passenger seat and kicked the door closed. "You did what? Diana..." He sounded as if he was exasperated with her. "And what is this girl going to be doing?"

Diana followed her husband in their warm and cozy house. Unzipping her coat, she lifted her sweater to nurse her son. She sat in the rocker as Danny sucked noisily and patted her breast with his hand, making it clear to his mama that he'd been put out. Diana toed off her boots and gazed up at the one man who still had the power to scramble all her reasonable thoughts with just a look. She loved this man more than her next breath. "I don't know, Jed. But she's got a little boy, and I overheard her in the grocery store, with a desperation I know, looking for a job. She looked so hungry. I took them for breakfast, too."

Diana held her breath, waiting for Jed to shout at her because, right now, they didn't have a plum nickel to spare. It was so tight, she had to be careful what she spent on anything, food, diapers, bargain shopping. She'd always been good at it, and now she was even better. Jed used every extra dime they had to outfit the necessary repairs to the barn, adding in three extra stalls just so they could get the therapeutic riding off the ground.

He set the bags on the table and walked across the floor until he was standing right in front of her, looking down on her. He took off his ratty cowboy hat and ran his fingers through his wavy brown hair. "Diana, I know you better than I think you know yourself. You may as well tell me all of it, because I also know that once you've made up your mind about something, nothing will change it. You've got a good heart, but you can't save the world, baby."

The way he said it had her eyes filling with tears as she rocked Danny and he continued to nurse. Jed pulled the padded stool for the rocker over and sat on it right in front of her and reached over, lifting Diana with Danny in her arms onto his lap. She leaned her head against his shoulder and he slid his arms around her, across the side of her thigh, possessively.

"I love you. I'm sorry…. I know we can't afford it, but I couldn't leave her. Who was going to help her?" Her voice caught when her husband sighed.

He tilted up her chin, the baby still latched on, and kissed her. "So, when does she start?"

Diana let out a sigh, and a tear slipped out as she stared into his amazing deep brown eyes, which said everything to her of how much she meant to him. "I love you."

"Yeah, well, that's a good thing, since we're well on our way to the poor house."

Danny took that opportunity to squeal and smack his lips, milk dribbling from his mouth.

"Jed, I'd go anywhere with you, as long as we're together." She leaned against her husband and gazed at her baby, unable to shake her worry for a young girl named Laura and the child she seemed to love so much.

CHAPTER 10

Andy sat in his truck, gazing out the window at the acres of pasture, the corral, the barn, just staring into the miles of forest that backed onto their land. A tap on the window had him sitting up, turning the key so he could roll down the window.

"Everything okay, boss?" asked Ben, the young stable hand, with auburn curly hair.

Andy opened his door and stepped out. He could feel Ben watching him as he stared at the back door. Ben cleared his throat, and Andy said, "Fine, Ben. Did you get those stalls cleaned out?"

"Almost done, sir," he said eagerly.

"Well, get to it," he snapped, heading toward the back door and dreading each step the closer he got. He listened to the gravel crunching under his booted feet. He rubbed his hand over his face.

He stepped inside and wiped his feet on the mat. This was probably the first time he'd ever been so meticulous. He was stalling and he knew it as he stepped to the kitchen door and took a breath, then another before pushing open the door and taking in the dinner-hour chaos. Food covered the counter, steam rose from the stove, and Jules, Aida, and three other servants all stopped and stared at him.

It was Jules who spoke first. "Sir, is there something I can get for you?" He didn't miss how nervous she was, and then she pointed to the door.

Andy ignored Jules and said, "Everyone, out. I need to talk to Aida." He didn't really care how he sounded, because he was worried how Aida would react to what he had to tell her about Laura. The fact was that Andy had screwed up, and he dreaded telling the one person with the gumption to stand up to him the way she did. To Andy, well, Aida mattered because of that.

The other servants left, but Jules stopped in front of him, wringing her hands. "Sir, your mother is entertaining through the holidays, and this is not the time to lose the cook...."

"Jules," Andy interrupted in a sharp voice he couldn't hide if he wanted to, "leave us now!"

Jules' face tinged pink, and she nodded, skirting around Andy and leaving the kitchen. Aida glanced up at Andy and then continued rolling out pastry dough. She said nothing but pursed her lips, her face taking on a hardness he didn't want to see.

"Aida, I went to Laura's today. And she was gone."

"Gone where?" She kept rolling the dough and then lined a pie plate. There were seven lined up.

"I don't know. That dump she lived in, the scumbag who owns it was there. He threw her out, said she couldn't pay the rent. The lady upstairs said Laura loaded her car last night and she hadn't seen her since." Andy rested his hand on the counter, waiting for the woman to start yelling, to say she quit, to call him a pig. Anything.

Instead, she calmly laid down the rolling pin and looked up at Andy with a hint of sadness in her eyes. "Did you know that girl is from Arlington? She got herself in trouble at fifteen, pregnant. Her parents threw her out when they found out. They didn't want her influencing her siblings with her seedy behavior, as they worded it, or rather, her mother did. Her father just turned his back on her. They said she was a bad influence and didn't want her around as a role model. All that girl did was have a momentary lapse, and, unlike many teens, she got pregnant. The boy, the father, treated her like a leper and would have nothing to do with her or the baby. So, with no money, she lived in a shelter in Arlington during the day, working part time at a fast food restaurant until the baby was born. But the social workers were sniffing around, looking to take her baby, and when she went into labor, the hospital notified social services because she was so young, and the social workers flocked in like vultures.

"She called her parents, but her mother said to her that if she wanted to come home, she'd have to give up the baby. Less than twelve hours after she gave birth, she walked out of the hospital with her baby and never looked back. She's been living here ever since. Do you know what that kind of fear and constant worry whispering in your ear does to a person? Gabriel is hers. She is young. She is honest. And that girl works harder than anyone I know and doesn't complain about anything. Working for a pittance, barely getting by, I think. Oh, she'd not speak of it. But I knew. I had eyes and could see the strain, the stress that she'd always cover up with a smile. But she was also beaten down. She had to shake off your daddy's advances more than once."

Aida watched him closely, but Andy was speechless and

didn't know what to say. Hearing that his dad had hit on Laura had a rage building to a slow boil inside him. He wanted to hit something. Maybe that was what she saw when he swiped his hand roughly over his face.

"Andy Friessen, maybe there is hope for you. But there is a difference, too, between being angry about someone wronged and doing something about it. So what do you plan on doing?"

She watched him closely, her arms crossed, and at any moment Andy half expected her to toss her apron and stomp out the door, telling him to shove this job. He could see the stubborn stance written all over her. All the years she'd worked for his family, he'd never really known her, which was a pity. He liked all of her "Right is right, and wrong is wrong" stance. It was refreshing to meet someone who didn't give a crap about what everyone thought or go along just because it was easier.

"I'll find her," he promised, but he was unsure of where to start and unwilling to admit even to himself that he needed to find Laura and her little boy for his own peace of mind. No one deserved how she had been treated.

Aida nodded. "Then you'd best go find her." She picked up the rolling pin and set about making her pies. "Now get out of my kitchen, Andy Friessen."

CHAPTER 11

It had been a long, cold night. Gabriel had whimpered off and on as the rain pounded the roof of the car. After their breakfast with Diana, Laura had been overwhelmed by her generosity and the fact that she had a full stomach, but that wouldn't keep Gabriel satisfied for long. As far as food, she didn't have much left. Gabriel had finished off the last of the bread and crackers. Laura nibbled on a cracker, hoping that would keep the hunger at bay. Finding a bathroom and a tap to get fresh water had been difficult. She had only one water bottle, so she was constantly having to refill it, and in a town as small as North Lakewood, it was difficult finding different public bathrooms. Maybe that was why, the fourth time she went into the older gas station and asked for the restroom key, the middle-aged guy behind the counter asked, "That your car parked around back?" and gestured with his head in a way that let her know he wasn't going to give her a break.

"Yes, sir." Her voice had been shaking even though she was so tired that all of her nerve endings were numb.

He jerked his thumb sideways. "Move it. This ain't a

hotel." He did, though, slide the key across the counter. "This is the last time you use the bathroom, too." He stared at her with a hardness in his eyes, and she truly understood his meaning.

She swallowed hard. "Thank you" was all she could say as she accepted the key and slunk around the outside of the old concrete building to the locked door of the filthy bathroom. After she was done, she pulled out her wallet, fingering ten dollars and handing it to the attendant.

"I need gas," she said. He took the money, and she was soaked from the rain by the time she put the gas in her car. She started the car and drove to the large mall outside town, parking at the far edge of the parking lot for the night. By this time, the temperature had dropped, and their clothes were damp, even what was in the trunk. Laura shivered while holding her son, wrapping him in blankets throughout the night.

Now, as daylight crept up, filling the gray skies, the rain had finally turned to a light drizzle. It would be hours before the mall opened, before she could find a bathroom, and, with the food gone, Laura realized she would have to use the last of her money to buy some. The thirteen dollars in her pocket wouldn't go far, and she worried and wondered, making a list of what food items she could buy that would be the cheapest. Milk was out, and so was cheese, bread only if there was something on sale. Fresh fruit and vegetables, forget it. That had never really been in the budget. Maybe she'd get lucky and find another jar of peanut butter marked down.

There was something about being cold and hungry that was humbling and brought her down to a level she never expected. But poor was poor. She wondered through the long night as she slept in fits, her legs cramping where her son lay across her lap, her neck pinched and stomach growling from hunger, how she'd dig them out of this mess. But there was a light on the horizon, and her name was Diana, and she'd meet her this morning outside the grocery store. So, with that thought to comfort her, she closed her eyes, pushing away the discomfort, and counted. It was only a few more hours. That was all she had to last before the mall opened and Laura would have to move her car.

There was a tapping on the window that brought Laura from a fitful sleep. She blinked and banged her head on the side window. Gabriel was still asleep, and Laura blinked and glanced up at the large figure outside her fogged-up window. She opened her door and lifted Gabriel off her lap, letting him stretch out on the cluttered backseat. A man wearing a black coat and a deputy's hat rested a large hand on the door and peeked in. Laura stepped out and shut the door.

"You been sleeping in your car, ma'am?" He didn't appear that old, with his light complexion, and there was a hint of concern in his eyes.

"Yes, sir. We just stopped here tonight." Laura was trembling inside and wondered if she'd get in trouble for parking where she did. She was unclear on the rules.

"How old's your boy?" He gestured with a slight tilt of his head.

"Gabriel is four." Laura gripped her shaking hands, wondering if she'd ever shake the chill that had soaked into her bones.

"Do you have a home? Or are you living in your car?" His tone, although sympathetic, was all cop, and that scared the hell out of her.

Her overtired head was scrambling to come up with something so they could slip away. He must have sensed it, as he unclipped the radio attached to his jacket and said, "Dispatch, I need you to send another car out to the mall and call social services."

That was all Laura needed to hear for her to frantically yank open the door and bump the deputy's leg, but he grabbed her around the waist and slammed her face down across the trunk.

"Settle down, or I'm going to slap the cuffs on you!" he yelled at her.

Gabriel started crying inside the car.

"Please, let me up. I need to get my son."

The deputy gripped her elbow and let her up. "Ma'am, you can open the door, and then you and your son are going to sit in the back of my car."

Laura felt as if the ground had disappeared beneath her. Her eyes burned, and as she glanced up, the deputy blurred. The back door opened, but Laura operated in a fog, unsure if it was the deputy who opened the door or if she had. His hand remained on her shoulder. Gabriel reached for her and wrapped his tiny arms around her neck, his legs around her waist, and the deputy led them to his car, opening the back door.

"Wait inside here." He shut the door. Even though the car was warm, Laura trembled.

She didn't wait long, gripping Gabriel so hard he fussed and pushed away. "Sorry, baby...." He gazed up at her, whining and pulling at her coat. A second cop car pulled up, another brown vehicle behind it. Her door opened, and there stood the sheriff, a blond, solid guy watching her with a mix of concern and resignation.

Laura saw another man dressed in a sloppy, heavy brown jacket and wool hat step out of the sedan. He was a little overweight, and he hadn't shaved. He had heavy bags under his eyes as he came closer and said, "Has anyone talked to her. What's the story?"

The first deputy replied, "Found her sleeping with the kid in the car. Thought I'd wait for you."

The sheriff shrugged. Laura didn't know where to look or who to look at. The older guy in the jacket leaned down in the open door.

"Are you in trouble, honey?"

Laura tried to speak but couldn't find her voice past the lump jammed in her throat, so she shook her head.

"What's your name?" he asked.

"Laura." She didn't recognize her own voice, barely a whisper.

"I'm Hank. I'm a social worker with the county."

Laura froze. She already suspected that was who he was, but hearing it made it real. She knew what this meant, and she also knew she was boxed in, as if she'd just been dumped down a hole with no way out.

"Look, I've done nothing wrong. We shouldn't have parked here, and if you'll let us go, we'll move on. I was tired, so we stopped. I thought it would be okay." She was so panicked she didn't know what she was saying.

The men exchanged a look. The social worker spoke up. "How old are you?"

"Twenty." She couldn't get her mind to work to say anything else.

"Is this your child, and where are you living?"

"Gabriel is my son." She didn't want to tell him she was homeless. She wanted to lie so they could get away and hide, except he must have known, all of them, as the sheriff leaned in next.

"I've seen you around town. Did something happen. A boyfriend? A bad relationship?" the sheriff asked.

Laura swallowed. "No. I lost my job and couldn't pay rent. I just got another one yesterday. I start today. I'll..." Laura stopped because she was babbling and didn't know what she was saying. Her head ached and she found it so hard to breathe. At this point, she didn't know what she was going to do. She wasn't one of those women who'd ever been able to lie her way out of a situation.

The social worker frowned and shook his head. "We can't let you stay out here. I'm going to have to take your son and put him in emergency care until you can get a home."

"No... you're not taking my son. Please just let me make a call," she cried. "Please don't take him. I have a job. I start today. I'm meeting her at the grocery store.... Please just let me call her. I'll see if she can help me, and I'll find a place today." She was begging, and Gabriel was shrieking, clutching her coat, his innocent eyes filled with a pool of tears.

"Sheriff." The social worker stood up, and the sheriff leaned in. A hand gripped her arm, pulling her up. Another hand grabbed her shoulder while one of them wrenched Gabriel from her arms. She heard Gabriel screaming as he reached frantically for her, but the social worker hurried away with him while the sheriff held on to her, his arm around her waist. She must have kicked him—she flung her arms, and the next she knew, she was face down on the trunk of the car, metal cuffs pinching her wrists. She couldn't breathe. Her nose was plugged, and her tears fell as she heard the car drive away and her little boy, Gabriel, crying for her.

The deputy was talking, and the sheriff was, too. "Calm down. I'm going to take these off." One of them unfastened the handcuffs and let her up. She didn't know who was talking. She couldn't see. Her vision was blurred, and she felt emotionally zapped, as if her skin had been peeled back, leaving her nerves raw and exposed as her heart snapped in two. "You can get him back. Just get a job. Get a decent roof over your head and enough money so you can feed your kid, and then contact Child Services. You'll get a hearing, and then you can apply to get him back."

"Why'd you take him? I'm his mother. Why?" she screamed, over and over.

"We take protection of a minor seriously, ma'am. You need to stop and think about your child. He's going to get fed; he'll have a warm bed to sleep in tonight." Before the sheriff left, he handed her the social worker's card. "He said to give you this. You can call him, and you need to move your car. Do you have gas in it, does it run?"

She nodded. That was all she could do, she was shaking so hard. She strode to the driver's door and yanked it open, sagging onto the seat as if she were an old woman. This time, the deputy touched her shoulder as he held the top of her door.

"I'm sorry, ma'am. Are you okay to drive?"

Laura was not going to look at him. At this moment, she hated him as she had hated no one before, and she said, in a voice that was so cold she felt chilled just speaking, "I'm fine." Pulling the door closed, she started her car. It backfired and slowly revved, as if deciding whether it would sputter and die or keep going. She knew they watched and waited until she drove through the parking lot to the north exit, where she paused, not sure which way to go. Then, she flicked on her signal light and turned right.

CHAPTER 12

Diana checked the time on her cell phone again—it was after nine. She was parked in front of the grocery store, and for the last ten minutes she'd waited on the sidewalk in front of the glass doors, walking in circles. Now, she leaned against the front of Jed's truck, thankful the rain had tapered off. She looked up and down the empty street for Laura but saw no one. The young grocery clerk, the same one from yesterday, wearing the same white and orange uniform shirt, waved to Diana from the storefront window and then frowned. Diana waved back. The girl gestured at her, and Diana realized she was obviously wondering why she was standing outside the store as if she were a teenager, loitering.

Diana held her cell phone in her right hand. She glanced at the time again. It was almost nine twenty-five, and still no Laura. What the hell had happened to her? Diana considered herself a good judge of character, so she couldn't understand why she wouldn't show up. She'd been desperate yesterday. She saw the way she worried over her small child; she knew how hungry they were.

She also knew she couldn't wait much longer, because Jed was waiting for them at home with Danny, who'd nursed just before she left. She hadn't pumped any milk to leave for him this morning, so regardless of whether she wanted to or not, she had to go. She called Jed, and he answered on the second ring.

"Yeah?"

Diana wanted to smile at her husband, who refused to get newer phones with call display. He never knew who was calling, but Jed could be quite prickly, and he said he just couldn't get people who screened their calls. It made no sense. If the phone rang, answer the damn thing.

"Jed, she's not here," she said, not knowing what to do and fearing she'd have to leave without her.

He sighed on the other end. "Diana, honey, you've got a heart of gold, but you can't help everyone. She obviously doesn't want help. Not everyone is made like you, honey."

"I know, but it still doesn't feel right. I understand that desperation... and what I saw in her yesterday..." Diana stopped as she glimpsed a thin woman wearing a dark coat and wool cap limping toward the store.

"Diana, are you there?" Jed said on the other end of the phone.

She pressed the cell phone to her ear, distracted. "Jed, I've got to go. I think I see her, but she's alone."

"Diana, you call me right back and let me know you're on your way home." She didn't miss the worry in his voice.

"I will. I love you." She hung up, knowing Jed would be in her SUV in five minutes unless she called back. He would drive faster than he should into town to rescue her, even if she wasn't in trouble. It was truly comforting to know that the one person she shared everything with, her heart, her soul, always had her back without question.

Diana tucked her phone in her pocket and hopped up on the sidewalk, walking toward the girl who stumbled toward her. "Laura?" She moved cautiously when she saw her pale face and her eyes, filled with something that reminded Diana of lost hope, as if she'd just lost every reason to live. It was a pain, an agony Diana had seen before—had lived before.

Laura gazed at her, unseeing, her eyes red rimmed and glossy. She opened her mouth, and her lips trembled.

"Laura, where is your son? Where is Gabriel?" Diana felt bone-chilling fear beating like wings up her spine when the girl's big, startled eyes gazed out at her as if she were the girl's only chance, and a thin chance it was.

The girl sagged, and Diana grabbed her shoulders, but she couldn't hold her up, so she sat her gently on the ground. Diana's phone rang in her pocket, and she knew it was her husband before she even answered.

"Jed." She stood up and touched her head, looking at the girl on the ground at her feet, who was just sitting there as if she'd lost her mind.

"Diana, what the hell is going on?" He was worried, and it always came across as irritation.

"I don't know, Jed, but something's happened. Her son's gone. She's sitting on the ground here." Diana knelt down and touched the girl's shoulder.

"I'm on my way. Stay put." He hung up, and she knew he'd be there in no time with her baby boy.

She glanced up to see a couple watching—gawking was more like it. Someone else was watching from the store window, and Mr. Harris, too, but no one came out to help. Diana urged the girl up, taking her elbow and moving her toward the truck. It took effort, and when she opened the passenger door, she leaned Laura against the truck.

"Can you sit in the truck? Come on, Laura, up."

Laura climbed in while Diana held her arm, but she still hadn't spoken. At least now she was out of view. The last thing Diana needed was to be the latest gossip, both her and Laura. She knew there'd be talk now, but if the girl kept sitting there, crying with Diana, the talk and the stories would be so much worse. She touched Laura's hand. It was pink and very cold. The girl was trembling and didn't respond to her touch.

"They took Gabriel. I shouldn't have stopped there," she whispered. "I tried to tell them I have work, but they still took him."

Diana felt the ground sway as if she were the butt of a cruel joke. But the joke apparently was on Laura. "What are you talking about? Who took Gabriel?"

Laura gazed up. Her eyes were dimmed, and the tiny spark of hope that had shimmered yesterday while she sat across the table from Diana at the diner had disappeared. "A deputy called a social worker and took him away from me. I don't know what to do."

Diana gaped and then turned her head when a vehicle's tires screeched. It was Jed, and he pulled in right beside the open passenger door of his truck and parked. He jumped out of the driver's seat; Danny was in his car seat in the back. In two strides, Jed was beside Diana, and he glanced at Laura, who appeared like an orphaned child.

"What's going on?"

Laura shrank back, and Diana didn't miss the fear. "Laura, this is my husband, Jed."

The girl gave a startled gaze like a spooked deer at Jed and then back to Diana. Diana held her hand and squeezed gently. "Jed, Laura said a deputy and a social worker took her little boy."

Laura gazed up at Jed, squinting as a hint of color dotted her cheeks. She quickly dropped her gaze, and Diana didn't miss how nervous she was around her husband. That was when it dawned on Diana, his resemblance to Andy.

"Laura, Jed is Andy's cousin, but they're not the same person. Jed, remember I told you last night that Laura used to work for Caroline, who fired her a few days ago?" She was trying to ease at least one worry from Laura. It just wasn't right to have the weight of the world on one's shoulders, and this girl seemed to have it all.

Jed exchanged a glance with Diana. "Laura, Caroline is a miserable person, and I'm sorry. I can only imagine how badly you were treated, but it sounds like you have a bigger problem: your son. So why did they take him?"

Laura's lips trembled, and when she glanced up sheepishly, she spoke softly. "We were sleeping in my car at the mall. The deputy who tapped on my window called the sheriff, and a social worker came. They said that when I have a job and a home, I can get him back." She reached into her pocket and pulled out a crumpled business card. She handed it to Diana with a hand that wouldn't stop shaking.

Diana read the name of Hank Walker, a social worker. She glanced at Jed, who leaned over her shoulder, reading the name as well.

"Laura, I'm going to call this social worker. We're going to get your son back." She glanced briefly at Jed, and he nodded.

Laura frowned. "How would you do that?"

"I'm a lawyer, but first we need to find out what happened." It was then that Danny started whimpering and fussing from his car seat.

"Diana, take the SUV, and take Laura home with you." Jed touched her shoulder.

Diana opened the back door. "Oh, baby, you lost your soother. Here it is." She put it in his mouth. "He's getting restless."

Jed helped Laura into the passenger seat of the SUV and hurried around to Diana before she slid in.

Diana touched his cheek when he leaned down and kissed her. "Where are you going?" She didn't miss the spark in his eyes.

"To pay the sheriff a visit," he said.

CHAPTER 13

Jed parked in front of the stone two-story building, the small city hall that the sheriff's office was in. He strode up the concrete steps two at a time and then went down the old tiled hallway to the double glass doors that read "Sheriff." He pushed them open and stopped at the front counter. A deputy with dark-rimmed glasses was behind the sterile brown counter. He glanced up at Jed.

"Is the sheriff in?"

The guy looked over his shoulder. "Can I tell him your name?"

Jed leaned his elbow on the counter. "Yeah. Jed Friessen."

The deputy picked up the phone and said, "There's a Jed Friessen here to see you, sir." He nodded and hung up the phone. "Go on back." He buzzed the gate. Jed pushed through, and the deputy pointed to an office at the back.

Jed knocked on the open door. "Sheriff?"

The blond-haired solidly built sheriff stood up and gestured to an empty chair at his desk. Jed closed the door.

The young sheriff sat back in an old wooden chair that squeaked and then leaned forward, resting his arms on the desk.

Jed sat and tilted back his hat. "You take a kid from a young lady named Laura?"

The sheriff didn't flinch but leaned back in the old swivel chair. The hinges squeaked again. "Yes. Are you related?"

"Why did you take her kid, Larry?" Jed asked.

The sheriff glanced at the door, and when he faced Jed, his baby blue eyes were hard and unforgiving. "We had a duty, Jed. My deputy found them living in her old car. She looks barely old enough to have a kid. It's damn cold out, and who knows how long they've been living like that and when the kid last ate?"

"She's at our place now. Diana hired her—she has a job. She'll have a place to live, too. So call this social worker and get her kid back to her." Jed hated this and watched as the sheriff shook his head.

"Doesn't work that way, Jed. This was an emergency situation. She'll have to contact social services, and there'll be a hearing to determine whether she has suitable living arrangements and whether she's fit as a parent. They'll investigate first, and then it'll go before a judge. It's not up to me anymore." He held up his hand when Jed cursed. "Hey... I am not about to allow some tiny kid to go back to that. If she's cleaned up and has a place, she'll get him back. But he's in the system now, and he's probably better off, too."

"In the system, are you kidding? What does that mean? Be honest, Larry. She's pretty torn up."

"Look. Your wife's a lawyer?" The sheriff wiped his hand across his face.

"Yeah, she's only done a few corporate things, wills, small stuff, nothing like this. She's helping me on the ranch and is a full-time mom." Jed never liked the fact that Diana worked, and he told her he'd provide—he'd look after them. He never wanted her to become a full-time lawyer in town and have Danny stuck with some nanny. It had been a bone of contention between them whenever clients phoned, because Jed was old school about a lot of things, including his opinion that a man should look after a woman, not the other way around.

The sheriff nodded. "So are you really taking this girl in and helping her?"

"Yeah, we are." Jed didn't know this girl from a hill of beans, but he trusted Diana and her instincts, even though he worried deep down that she'd be taken advantage of. But he had seen the girl with his own eyes—seen how torn up she was and how young she was. Before he got any deeper in with this girl, he was determined to find out more about her, and the entire situation, for his wife's sake.

The sheriff opened his top drawer. "Here's the social worker's card. Call him, tell him she wants to see him. She's entitled. Ask them to set up a hearing. And for God's sake, make sure she's got a roof over her head. Do you even know why she was on the streets?"

Jed didn't give too much away, so he took the card and said, "Thanks, Sheriff," and started to leave.

"What do you really know about this girl, Jed?"

Jed stopped with his hand on the door. "Why are you asking?"

"Maybe you should ask yourself if the kid isn't better in a foster home, where he can get three square meals and a warm bed to sleep in," the sheriff said none too lightly.

Jed opened the door. "What about love, Sheriff? You

forgot to mention that part. Diana will be calling. I expect you'll treat my wife with respect." He paused. The sheriff inclined his head. Jed left and was almost to his truck when someone shouted his name.

It was Andy, shouting out his open window, and he pulled in, parked beside Jed's truck, and jumped out. Jed shook hands with his cousin.

"What are you doing here?" Andy asked. "I've been meaning to call you to come out and see you, Diana, and that godson of mine."

Jed tilted his hat up. "Stopped in to talk to the sheriff."

Andy appeared distracted until Jed mentioned the sheriff. "Everything okay? Did something happen?"

"No, just some young girl Diana found yesterday with her kid in the store hungry. The sheriff took her kid away this morning. Diana was trying to help her after finding them...."

Andy cut him off before he could finish. "Was her name Laura, by any chance?"

Jed narrowed his eyes. "That's her. Guess you know her. Heard she worked for Caroline and she fired her."

Andy nodded. "I've been looking for her. She was fired by Mother in one of her fits. I was finding her another job, but I went to her place only to find out she'd been thrown out by her slime-bag landlord. So what happened, and where is she?" Andy sounded worried, and Jed really looked at him, because that was so unlike his cousin.

"Right now, Diana's taken her home. All I know is she's been sleeping in her car. The sheriff had social services take her kid. Diana found them yesterday, hungry, begging for a job at the grocery store. She took them to Merle's and fed them, offered the girl a job. She was supposed to meet her at nine outside the grocery store."

Jed watched Andy, wondering if he was sincere. After all, his history with women wasn't great. "Were you sleeping with her?"

Andy narrowed his eyes and snapped, "No, I wasn't."

"You know darn well why I asked. You and your daddy have a way with women, turning their lives upside down."

"I'm not my dad, Jed. You know that. And that girl didn't deserve to be treated that way."

Jed nodded, seeing a side of Andy he hadn't before. "Well, if you want to follow, I got to go tell my wife what the sheriff said. But I got to warn you, Laura was pretty messed up when Diana took her home."

Andy really did appear worried. His entire expression surprised Jed. "I'll be right behind you." Andy ran his hand over his head and then strode back to his truck and climbed in, following Jed back to his ranch.

Andy parked beside Jed's truck in front of his house. Diana must have seen Jed coming, as she was pulling on her coat as she closed the front door behind her, clipping the baby monitor to the waistband of her jeans. She hopped down the stairs and then paused mid-step when she saw Andy. Even though they'd come so far, the array of emotions that shifted through her face had Jed worrying about her still.

Jed leaned in and kissed his wife. He touched her cheek, taking in her softness and the tiny lines that seemed to have popped up overnight around her eyes. "Where's Danny, and Laura?"

Diana slid her hand in his, holding it a little tighter than usual. "Danny's sleeping. Just put him down. Laura fell asleep on the sofa. I made her eat some eggs and toast. I know she was starving," Diana said, as she stepped closer to Jed. He could see that this whole situation with Laura, and now with Andy here, was reminding her of things she most likely didn't want to remember.

Andy strode up. "Diana, I heard you found Laura."

Diana glanced briefly at Jed. Jed knew her concern. "He's been looking for her," he explained.

"Why were you looking for her, Andy? What do you want with her?" Diana asked in a way that was as fierce as a protective mama bear. Jed slid his arm around her and pulled her closer to him.

"She didn't deserve what happened. I was trying to find her another job. I promised the cook that I would. My intentions are honorable, nothing more. She's young, and I feel sorry for her to be treated so horribly. It was unfair what Mother did, and the cook told me a few things. Laura hasn't had an easy life..." Andy started, but he said no more, wondering if maybe he shouldn't repeat it. "I'd like to help if I can."

"She looks pretty young to have a kid, only twenty, so I can only imagine the story. It sounds as if you know more, Andy?" Diana slid her hand over Jed's chest as he kissed the top of her head.

Danny started whimpering from inside, and Jed slipped the monitor from Diana's waistband. "I'll get him." He reached in his pocket and pulled out a business card. "This is from the sheriff. He said to call this guy. He took the kid. He's the social worker."

Jed slid his hand around Diana's chin and watched her for a second until she looked up at him. He knew she'd be okay. He hurried to the door and hopped to the top step. When he slid open the door, Laura scrambled up off the sofa as if she'd just been caught doing something she shouldn't.

"Diana." Jed motioned her in with his hand. He knew she'd understand, as she opened her mouth and nodded.

"Would you like a coffee, Andy? I think Laura's awake." She tucked her hands in her pocket and went to Jed, who held out his hand to her.

"Sure," Andy replied, and he followed, determined. Jed could see the hesitation and something else in his cousin. For the first time, he appeared willing to help.

CHAPTER 14

Diana was an incredible woman, and as Andy watched his cousin, his godson, and the unspoken bond that linked them together, he realized it was envy that burned his heart, not jealousy. Jed made her happier than he'd ever seen, and he'd never seen Jed so head-over-heels in love with a woman as he was with Diana.

Laura on the other hand sat quietly in the corner, scared and weary. Her cheekbones seemed even more pronounced than before. Diana slid her arm around her waist and talked to her as she walked her down the hall for a shower and gave her a change of clothes. Laura was the same height as Diana but was much thinner, and Andy couldn't imagine what it was like to go without food as he realized she may have been starving herself, and it wasn't by choice. He'd never had to live hand to mouth and had wasted more than his fair share of food every day, which he was sure she would have gladly eaten. He wondered now as he watched her if any of their other staff were going hungry.

Andy had never given a second thought to those who

couldn't afford to feed themselves, and even though he realized and saw the hunger in Laura, not just for food but for her child, he wanted to tell her it would be okay, but the words fell short on his lips.

Andy paced the tiny living room while he listened to the shower just down the hall. Diana phoned the social worker before Laura got in the shower and left a message. She picked up the phone again and dialed, shrugging off her coat and dumping it on the kitchen chair.

"This is Diana Friessen. This is the second time I've called for Hank Walker. I am a lawyer representing Laura Parnell...." Diana let out a sigh of frustration and held the phone away from her ear. "I'm on hold again," she muttered. "Yes, Mister Walker, I'm Diana Friessen. I am a lawyer representing Laura Parnell. You took her son, Gabriel, from her this morning in a shopping mall parking lot. They were in their car."

Diana picked up a pen from the table and sat down, sliding her open notebook towards her and pointing her pen to handwritten notes. "Look, my client would like to see her son." Diana started scribbling something below all the notes she'd written and then shook her head and appeared irritated, as if something the man was saying was making her angry.

"I understand how it works, but keeping a child from his mother is not okay. She has every right to see him."

"What?" she barked into the phone, and Jed started hovering, his hands on his hips. Andy was pretty sure that if the man on the end of the line were in the room, Jed would be having a word with him about not upsetting his wife. "I have never heard anything so ridiculous: getting him settled, giving him time to settle in. What the hell kind of ridiculous system are you running? He misses his mother. He wants to see her. You're wrong; kids don't just settle…"

He must have cut her off, as Diana slapped her hand on the table and stared at Jed with a fire in her eyes that made Andy pretty sure she was holding back a few choice words for this worker.

"I want an emergency hearing scheduled for my client. You had no right to take her child the way you did. She has a job and a place to stay now…"

The man must have cut her off again.

"Well, you make sure you get back to me today." Diana hung up the phone. The long cord was stretched from where she sat.

"Well?" Jed asked.

Diana scribbled something down on the page of notes and then dropped the pen on the table. "That prick is stonewalling me." She then pulled out her day timer and started thumbing through a list of phone numbers.

"What are you doing?" Jed asked as he hovered over Diana.

"Someone I went to law school with. I know he's with a firm in Seattle. He specialized in cases like this, family law. I'm going to call him." Diana dialed the rotary phone.

"Could be here a while, Andy," Jed said. "You want some coffee?"

Andy shrugged and followed Jed into the tiny kitchen. Jed finished pouring a cup for Diana and set it in front of her, and he leaned in and kissed her as she waited on hold again.

Andy poured his own cup and walked around the corner into the tiny living room, Jed with him. "Sounds like Diana's getting jerked around. Do you want me to call my lawyer? He can make things happen."

"I don't want any help from you."

Andy hadn't heard Laura approaching, but there she stood in the cluttered hallway of this small bungalow, her eyes red and her wet hair combed and hanging straight down her back. She was wearing a pink sweat suit that looked two sizes too big for her. Her face was thinner, drawn, as if she'd lost another few pounds while showering, and she stared at Andy with so much anger she was shaking. "I needed that paycheck to pay my rent, to buy food. I was sent away with nothing. Your mother saw fit to keep it, so I don't want your help."

Jed stepped around Andy and right into Laura's space like he would a horse that was so spooked it would most likely bolt. "Laura, don't put that on Andy. That's not fair. He's been looking for you to find you another job. He even went to where you lived, and you were gone."

For the first time, Andy was ashamed of where he came from. "Laura, what my mother did was not okay. And you're right: Maybe it was my fault."

She stared at him with hatred. "You're damn right it was. I was so tired of the bullshit between you and your mother. She demanded the tree go in your library, and you yelled to get rid of it, and then you sat there watching me, just like your daddy, as if you expected me to just lie on my back and spread my legs for you. I just wanted a job with peace so I could feed my son. And now he's gone." She was crying again.

Diana hung up the phone and hurried over to Laura, wrapping her arms around the girl, hugging her. "Oh, Laura, it's okay, but blaming Andy isn't going to solve anything. He really was trying to help you. Now, come sit down. I've just contacted another lawyer I know in Seattle, and he's sending me the forms to file for an emergency hearing. He's going to walk me through the process. Andy, I did hear you offer your lawyer's help. Family law's not my specialty, but I could use the resources, if your lawyer would be willing." Diana led Laura to the kitchen table. "Laura we will get your son back, and we're going to use all the help we can get."

"Consider it done. Whatever you need, I'll call them and get the ball rolling." Andy took a step toward Diana and Laura, cutting his hand in the air, but this time, Laura refused to look at him.

"I have to go check the horses, Andy." Jed motioned to the door. Diana and Laura sat at the table. Ever so slowly, Laura looked up at him and just stared and frowned. Not a spark of life appeared in those mesmerizing green eyes.

"Okay." Andy opened the door, and Jed followed. As he strode beside Jed to the barn, Andy couldn't help feeling responsible for this mess. The way Laura had looked at him with such hatred, it tore at his heart, and he wanted to shake her, to make it right, to go and get her kid for her, just so some of the life he knew was there deep inside of her would return to those amazing green eyes.

Jed must have sensed this, as he gripped his shoulder. "It's not your fault."

"Well, that's the thing. It is partly my fault. I made a promise to someone, and I dropped the ball." Jed stopped and watched him just outside the barn, saying nothing. At times like this, Andy thought his silence was unnerving, the way Jed could read people and look into his soul and call out all his bullshit. "I got a call to make for your wife. At least I can do that much." Andy walked away with the cell phone pressed to his ear and Jed's all-knowing gaze burning a hole in his back.

CHAPTER 15

It had been a long day. Andy contacted his lawyer, who brought in Ed Turner, an associate in their family law department. It was twenty minutes later that Ed phoned Diana and had her on the phone for an hour, scribbling notes furiously.

It was getting late, and he could see Diana winding down. He needed to get back to the estate. He picked up his coat and watched Laura, who sat in the corner of the sofa with Danny in her lap as if he gave her some peace.

"Leaving?" Jed asked as he slid his hand over Diana's shoulder and then rubbed both as if they were stiff.

"Yeah, I have to get back."

Diana hung up the phone before Andy could step out the door. "We got it, yeah." She threw her hands in the air and then patted Jed's hand on her shoulder.

"Your lawyer—thank you, Andy—arranged for a visitation tomorrow and an emergency hearing in forty-eight hours, but with Christmas a week away, the courts are going to shut down for the holiday season. He had me on the phone while he arranged all this. He's good, by the way.

One of his arguments was 'What could be worse than separating a mother and child at Christmas?' I'm hopeful now." Diana slid around and said to Laura, "Don't lose hope. We're getting him back, but I need to go over some things with you." Danny was rubbing his eyes and started fussing. "And I need to start dinner."

"And you need to feed Danny, and you need to take a break for a bit, too, Diana." Jed jabbed his finger at her. "I'm just going to walk Andy out. I'll help get dinner started after I get back in." Jed followed Andy out into the dimming light.

"Jed, let me give you some money for Laura to look after her." Andy started to reach into his pocket to pull out his wallet.

"You know better than that. I'm not taking money to look after Laura. You may need to settle up with her for other things, her job and all that, but you need to work it out with her," Jed sighed and glanced back at the house.

"You really don't like Diana working, do you?" Andy said. He watched his cousin, who wore the expression of a man struggling to come to terms with something.

"Nope, but she needs to do this for Laura. I understand that, I get that, but I don't like it, because she'll put everything she's got into it, still giving to me and to Danny, and leave nothing for herself. That's the way she is. She takes on other people's hurt, and it'll end up destroying her. So no, I don't want her working. I want her here so I can look after her," Jed said as he gazed back at the house.

As Andy drove back to the estate, he understood, in a way, Jed's need to protect Diana. He loved her so much, and he also saw in Diana what Jed mentioned. He wondered if she could ever get past that powerful trauma she had endured as a child, which had shaped her into who she was and defined how she handled everything in her future. Then he wondered about Laura and what Aida had said. At fifteen, sixteen, he couldn't have imagined surviving on his own, let alone caring for an infant.

Andy had just parked his truck when Jules popped open the back door in a freshly pressed black dress with a white apron fitted over the front. The way she scurried toward him was like nothing he'd ever seen. Waves of anger and irritation were rolling off her as if she'd been standing at the door watching for him. He absolutely hated anyone doing that to him.

"Jules," Andy said, annoyed.

"Sir, you don't answer your phone anymore? Your mother is fit to be tied. You are supposed to be Miss Johnston's escort for dinner tonight. Your mother..." She was right beside him, carrying on like one of those annoying Chihuahuas.

Andy cut Jules off before she could continue: "I'm not interested in my mother's tantrums, and I have better things to do than escort some pretty rich bitch like the two of us are on display. Is Aida around?"

Jules sputtered. "Mister Friessen, Andy... what am I supposed to tell your mother? She ordered me to track you down." Andy glared at Jules until she stepped back and said, "The cook is in the kitchen."

Andy started toward the back door, then stopped when he could hear Jules' ragged breathing. "Jules, tell my mother I'm here and that I told you I'll talk with her shortly."

"Yes, sir." She nodded, and her face softened as if some of her stress had left.

"Oh, and Jules?" Andy set his hands on his hips.

"Yes, sir?"

"I want you to make sure that from now on, the staff, and I mean everyone, are fed."

Jules frowned and stared at him, confused. "I don't understand, sir?"

"For one, I guarantee the amount of food for all these parties my mother is planning would feed the entire community. Make sure the staff, anyone who wants to, takes what's left and nothing's wasted. Every day, Jules, see to it that everyone who comes to work here gets a meal."

Jules said not one word as she stared at him with an expression he'd never seen before. "As you wish, sir."

Andy stepped inside and found the cook in the kitchen. She was giving orders to half a dozen staff members, all dressed in black and white, with starched collars and bow ties. Food, platters, and bowls covered the counters. Pots steamed on the stove. When Aida's eyes met Andy's, she said in an abrupt tone, "Everyone, out."

As soon as the last staff member left and the door closed, Andy said. "Laura is at my cousin Jed's. Something's happened, Aida."

She rested her hands on the counter. "Oh? And what happened?" She said it in a way that sounded fed up and just plain tired.

"She was sleeping in her car, and a deputy found her at the mall. The sheriff called social services, and they took her son away."

"Oh, no!" Aida cried out and pressed her hand to her heart. "That poor girl! After all she fought and struggled through to keep him with her, it just ain't right."

"Aida, we're getting him back. Diana's a lawyer, and I've already contacted mine, and they're working with her."

"But how long will that take? Separating a mother and

child at Christmas just isn't okay. And once your child is gone, it ain't that easy to get him back."

"Aida, I promise you that I'll make sure it happens."

She stared at him for a few seconds, long and hard, and then walked away. "Then you'd best get on with it. Now get out of my kitchen, Andy Friessen."

Andy watched Aida for a moment, her back ramrod straight as she lifted something hot and heavy from the oven. He sensed that Aida was counting on him, but at the same time she was watching him. It was disconcerting having that put on you, especially from someone who mattered. And Aida mattered.

Andy pushed open the kitchen door, nearly tripping over Jules and the wait staff who hovered just outside, the same staff Aida had kicked out of the kitchen moments ago. He stared at them, and then down at Jules, who was looking at him now as if he'd lost his mind. Andy pushed past them and hurried upstairs for the first time ever, realizing he had made a promise he might not be able to keep, and that just didn't sit right.

CHAPTER 16

Guests mingled in the library, the living room, and the grand foyer of the estate as waiters in white shirts and bow ties carried trays of hors d'oeuvre and glasses filled with champagne. His mother had outdone herself this year, and the house was decorated in all manner of Christmas glory. Christmas lights stretched up the entire long driveway to the estate. For the first time ever, Andy wondered about the extravagance of the electricity bill. He'd never thought of it before, but all the finery, the food, the liquor that would go to waste tonight would feed so many hungry families. He just hoped that the staff took what was left of the food after the party, because he knew most of it would get dumped in the trash otherwise.

"There you are, darling." Caroline slid her arm through Andy's, and she patted his black tailored tux, which had been imported from some fancy Parisian outfit and cost more, he realized, than what Laura paid for rent in a year.

Andy glanced at his mother, dressed in a silver sequined gown, her hair curled, just touching her shoulders, perfectly groomed and not a hair out of place. She flashed a tasteful amount of diamonds: earrings, necklace, and a bracelet. Again, he couldn't help wondering how the value of one ring could set Laura and her son up for life.

"What's going on in that head of yours, Anderson?" She smiled and flicked her fingers at the senator, who was speaking with Todd. Alexis stood beside her father, and their gazes met for a second. Then she looked away and smiled and laughed at something Todd said.

"Nothing, Mother. So how long are you going to hold me hostage here?" he snarled, wanting to burst out the back door, squealing down the driveway and out of there.

She grinned, flashing perfectly straight white teeth. Her icy blue eyes were free of any loving motherly concern. "You have two choices here, darling, and only one is the right one. So I suggest you put on that dashing smile of yours and go over to woo Alexis. So far, all you've managed to do is irritate her, and that is making the senator unhappy. Since your father and I were just speaking of your cousin Jed and the money he needs to get that therapeutic riding off the ground, we've told the senator how supportive you are of the venture and how interested you are in his daughter. He wants this alliance as much as we do. Now smile. I'm sure your father has talked to you."

Andy stared at his mother. "If you think threatening to take funding away from Jed is going to make me toe the line, you're sorely mistaken. There are other avenues for Jed, and I'll make sure to help him."

His mother laughed, a very ladylike soft chuckle that drove a shiver up his spine. "Oh, Anderson, without the senator's help, it's not just funding. You should know better than anyone that there is also licensing approval, and from what I understand, they have to be careful nowadays with anyone who wants to work with children, especially those with special needs. After all, who knows what people really have hidden away in their closets, what can suddenly creep out with further investigation?" His mother patted his arm. "Now, I think Alexis is looking a little warm. Maybe she could use a refreshment and you could show her the sunroom."

At one time, Andy had protected his family, their reputation. He had done things to clean up the messes his father was constantly in. He knew his father loved him, but his mother... he wondered what the woman was really about.

Maybe it was her insinuated threat to Jed's future that had him walking toward the senator and his daughter. Whatever it was, the seed she'd planted of the chaos she could unleash had him pulling back in this fight again. If there was one thing he had learned in business and in fighting, it was to know his opponent, to know his weakness, and to never take on a fight he couldn't win.

"Senator Johnston, so glad you could come." He gripped the man's hand. He was tall and solidly built, his graying hair and hazel eyes adding to his distinguished appearance. His hand rested on his daughter's back, and he eyed Andy in a way that told him that if he hurt his daughter, he'd destroy him.

"Alexis, you look lovely tonight." Andy had to dig deep to play the role his mother wanted, even though Alexis did look stunning in a deep blue gown that showed off her exquisite figure.

"Thank you, Andy. I must say, you clean up quite well yourself, but then, I wondered if you were going to show at all." She glared at him coolly, letting him know she wasn't fooled for one minute. She turned away. "Excuse me, I'm finding it a little stuffy. I think I'll get some air." She patted her father's arm. "I'll be back, Father."

"Andy, why don't you show Alexis the sunroom," Caroline stated as she walked up behind him, and she smiled at the senator. "We should really allow these two some time to get to know each other."

Andy gritted his teeth but stepped forward and offered his arm to Alexis. She had been raised with impeccable manners and understood society's rules, so she accepted his arm and walked with him.

"You know, Andy, I'm no fool. I know you're a smart man. You do realize your mother and my father would like nothing more than for us to be involved, for you to court me, shall we say. The only reason I was invited here was for us to have a chance to get to know each other. But I won't be played for a fool. You and I both know you have about as much interest in getting to know me as a cat does a dog."

Andy didn't much like being called out, but she had nailed what he was thinking on the head—and what he was feeling. He paused and lifted a glass of champagne off a tray of a passing waiter. "Alexis?"

She inclined her head and accepted the glass.

"Bourbon for me," Andy ordered to the young waiter. "Alexis, you'll love the view from this room." He escorted her down five steps and into a wide, open sunroom filled with plants, a corner pond, a rock wall fireplace and plush furnishings. Thankfully, it was empty of any guests.

Alexis strode to a bench seat beside the stone pond and dipped her hand in. "This is a lovely room; even the air is fresh in here." She didn't smile, but when she gazed at Andy, he noted a hint of sadness before the waiter returned with his bourbon. She dropped her gaze quickly, hiding it from him, and smiled, and all the control and strength of a woman in charge returned when she glanced back up with those hard blue eyes.

"Thank you." Andy lifted his glass to Alexis. "Merry Christmas, Alexis. You're right about one thing: I'm not interested in a relationship. I don't know you, and I have a lot I'm dealing with right now. So I apologize if you feel slighted."

Alexis slid around and sipped her champagne before setting the full glass beside her on a side table. "You do appear distracted. I'm not a monster, Andy Friessen. Maybe what you need is a friendly ear from someone who is impartial."

"Thank you. That's not what I expected, but maybe you can tell me what business your father has with mine right now?"

She never flinched when she said, "Well, your mother and my father have been in business together, but I know right now that my father and yours have investments in some offshore company. My daddy is ensuring that subsidies are provided and that the company's debt is forgiven. But aren't you already involved in the business part of this?"

Andy stared at this striking woman, wondering if she really understood what she'd said. "My father and I work closely together in business, but what you're talking about is fleecing the taxpayer while contributing nothing."

She tilted her head back and laughed. "Oh, Andy, you surprise me. Half the people at this party have built their wealth this way, from subsidies and forgiveness of debts so that they can buy more, invest more. After all, it's the American way."

Andy glanced at the crowd of family friends, guests just

outside the sunroom, all with wealth in some form. He realized he really didn't know how they'd made their money and, in that moment, felt something inside himself awaken. He realized the unbalance of it, the injustice, having more money than you needed. It was Laura's thin face that flashed before him and the screams of others from his past: the unseen, the impoverished, and those trying to make a difference. Andy never saw her get up, but she was in front of him, and she took his glass from his hand, set it on the wooden ledge beside him. Her hands clasped his waist, and she stepped closer, tracing a finger up his chest, over his chin and lips with her soft hands, her long red nails.

"I'd love to explore what could be, maybe get to know you a little better."

She smelled so sweet. He'd been a long time without a woman. She pressed her breasts into his chest and lifted her lips in offering. Andy didn't know why he did it—maybe curiosity had him lowering his head and tasting her and what she offered. He took advantage of her open mouth and probed with his tongue; he could feel her quiver and settle in closer, running her hand down his back, up over his shoulders. He moulded his mouth over hers with fierce pleasure. He began to breathe harder, faster, demanding more, which she willingly offered. Then he lifted her, pulling her closer, adjusting her hips against his. She locked her arms around his neck and squirmed.

A gasp sounded from behind him, and a woman squeaked. "Oh, excuse me!"

Andy pulled back, prying Alexis' arms from his neck. The woman quickly left. Alexis stared at him with a heavy-lidded gaze, her lips red and pouty. He needed to step back, get some air. He couldn't believe what he'd almost done.

"I'm sorry, Alexis, but I just realized I have someplace

else I have to be. I apologize for deserting you." He left shaking, gritting his teeth as he woefully fought to gain control, taking the back stairs two at a time up to his room, where he changed into something warm, something casual, and slipped out the side door.

CHAPTER 17

ndy had ignored the dozen or so calls buzzing from his cell phone, which lay on the leather passenger seat beside him. The phone had lit up minutes after he'd driven away from the estate. He knew who was calling: his mother, or rather, Jules, ordered by his mother. But Andy was having none of it. He realized then that he needed to do his homework and keep his distance from Alexis or she'd cloud his good sense and have him taking her to his bed, testing how wild she could be. He needed to stay focused because his father and Senator Johnston were up to something, and whatever it was meant billions and a union that would create a powerful dynasty. It always came down to money, power, and politics, but what Andy couldn't shake as of late was that the closeness he had once shared with his father had changed.

Clint, their family lawyer, met Andy at the Arlington office. Andy knew quite well he was walking a fine line, as Clint's representation included the whole family, his mother and father. Would he betray a confidence? He didn't think so, but he still needed to be cautious. Clint was brilliant, as were many of the lawyers on his staff. He had short, dark hair, a lean body, striking features, and he appeared born to wear the finest suits.

"So, what can I do for you?" Clint, dressed in dark slacks and a green sweater, sat in his dark leather chair.

"I wanted to touch base about Laura and the lawyer you assigned to help Diana with the upcoming hearing to get her child back." Andy wondered, by the way Clint watched him for a second before tapping a few keys on his computer keyboard, if he suspected that wasn't why he was really there, but he didn't know how to jump into *So what are my parents and the senator really up to?*

Clint read something on the screen before replying, "Everything's set. But you should know that it's unlikely she'll get her kid back before the holidays. Child Services takes every emergency situation seriously, and once they have your kid, you have to jump through a lot of hoops to get them back. Staying at her lawyer's house, which, from what I understand, is barely big enough to house Diana and Jed, isn't going to fly with any judge, let alone social services."

Andy wondered if Diana knew that Clint had information on her household.

"You know, Andy, your cousin and his wife, what they are doing is admirable. But without this girl having steady employment and a decent roof over her head, which is going to take some time... I hate to tell you this, but I wouldn't count on her getting him back until she has all these things in place. She's got too many strikes against her. She's only twenty, a relative minor, under the legal drinking age of this state. The court does take all that into consideration: age, wisdom, knowing the best for her child. She's barely getting by, forced to live on the street because she couldn't pay rent, couldn't feed her child. Child poverty is taken seriously, as is the fact that, through careless actions, she was fired with cause by your mother."

That last comment had Andy gripping the chair arms. "Where are you getting all this? First of all, what my mother did was unfair. That was not Laura's fault, and my mother withheld her salary..."

Clint cut him off. "For damages, which I understand doesn't begin to cover the cost. She's darn lucky your mother hasn't gone after her for the rest."

"What the hell, Clint? I was there. Where are you getting this from, anyway? My mother?" Andy pulled back when he realized Clint knew something that he wasn't telling. "You've talked to my mother, haven't you?"

"Look, Andy, I'm the family lawyer. Your father and mother are the heads of the household. I have a responsibility to report to them."

"What about lawyer-client confidentiality?" Andy didn't like where the conversation was headed when Clint sighed.

"Andy, your mother is my client." Clint tapped his fingers on the desk.

"Are you telling me you informed my mother of Laura's situation?"

Clint stared for a minute and then nodded. "I had a duty, Andy. So is there anything else I can help with tonight?"

"Yeah, you can tell my mother she can..." He stopped and stood. He knew better. Clint may have been their family lawyer, but Andy now knew where his allegiance lay. "You know what? Never mind. Thanks for coming in, Clint." He walked out the door and around the corner to the elevator and paused when he heard Clint speaking.

"He was just here. I told him.... Is there anything else you want me to do?"

Andy felt poleaxed; he knew Clint was on the phone. He didn't know who he was talking to, but he had a pretty good idea. He didn't linger when he heard the phone being hung up. What he did do was push open the door and take the stairs down to his truck, parked in the dark lot. He sat in his truck for a few minutes before starting it and pulling out. It was too late to go out to Diana and Jed's. They'd all be asleep, so he went home, but instead of going in, he went to the stables and lit up the round ring. He led Sugar, his Quarter Horse, into the ring and slid off her harness. She was still green and bucked and fought him in the ring when he first started. She was a challenge at times, and tonight he needed that perspective.

After he had her settled in a stall, brushed down and watered, he lingered in the barn until he could see many of the guests leaving. Then he snuck in a side door and up the stairs to his room. All night, he tossed around what to say to Diana, to Laura, to Jed, whether he'd tell Diana about his visit to Clint. But the next morning, as he pulled in to Jed and Diana's, he still didn't have a clue what to say.

Diana waved from the stables. Laura was in the corral, wearing a ratty brown coat and wool cap; she had rubber boots on her feet as she strode through the mud, dumping the contents of the bucket she carried into a wooden trough. She stared at Andy, her lips forming a thin white line.

"Good morning, Laura."

She turned her back. Andy couldn't remember the last time someone had viewed him with such hatred, and that bothered him. Usually, he didn't give a second thought to whether someone hated him. He knew that over the years he had made plenty of enemies, many of them women.

"What brings you out here this morning?" Jed strode out of the barn.

"Wanted to talk to your wife, if that's all right?" Andy said as he watched Laura latch the corral gate and enter the barn.

Jed followed his gaze. "Give her some time. She has a right to be angry with a whole lot of people, but she's confused on who's done what, so she's thrown you right into the mix. Diana's talking to her."

Andy stared at his cousin. "We may have a problem. I didn't sleep much last night after tossing around what my lawyer said."

"Oh, and what is that?" Jed stepped closer.

"Paid him a visit last night. He pretty much said she's not going to get Gabriel back now, that staying out here, crammed in with you two, won't help her case. She needs a job, a decent roof over her head." Andy stopped for some reason, not wanting to continue.

Jed, knowing him better than anyone, said, "There's more, isn't there? You may as well say all of it."

"My mother is up to something and may have her hand in this." Andy could feel Jed's gaze heating up, and his stance hardened. When he looked at Jed, he could see a tell-tale flush tingeing his cheeks. His cousin was furious, and when he was this mad, he became very quiet. "I don't know for sure, but my lawyer brought up my mother firing Laura for cause, and he said Laura was fortunate my mother didn't go after her for all the damages."

"What the hell, Andy? What did Laura do?" Jed growled.

"Well, that's the thing. It wasn't her fault. It was an

accident; she tripped and fell in the tree and knocked it over, breaking some crystal and spilling liquor on the carpet. I was the one who told her to get rid of the tree. I was angry at my mother for sticking it there in the first place." Andy watched as Laura strode out of the barn, pausing to stare at him before she hurried into the house and shut the door.

"There's one more thing. I didn't want to mention it," Andy said, and then he cleared his throat roughly when Jed's eyes darkened.

"Oh, and what is that?"

"You've applied for funding to start therapeutic riding for disabled kids?" Andy hesitated.

"Don't remember mentioning my business to you, Andy. So I guess you better tell me everything, because it sounds like someone's messing around in my affairs."

"My mother apparently has an agenda that focuses on me. Unless I make a plan to wed the senator's daughter, your funding is going to come under scrutiny. When I said that I can help you get what you need, she laughed and said something about licensing problems, that hidden skeletons have a way of popping up. Jed, you don't know my mother and her political connections." Andy wondered if he had done the right thing in telling Jed.

"So let me get this straight. Your mother is blackmailing you to manage your personal affairs. She's looking for your weakness, which, let's say, is me. And let's say that the reason for you to marry this powerful senator's daughter is the heart of the matter. Have you figured out what your mother's getting out of this?"

"Oh, yeah. Other than a powerful political ally, this is about good old-fashioned money and power," Andy said.

Jed shook his head. "I'm the wrong man to mess with.

You better go talk to Diana, but don't mention the funding for the therapeutic riding. This is Diana's dream, to help kids without a voice, and I'll walk through hell to make sure her dream becomes a reality. Do you understand?"

Something passed between them, a trust that hadn't been there before with Diana, and Andy understood Jed's need to protect her. He inclined his head and walked into the barn. Diana was in a stall with Scarlett, her dark Quarter Horse, grooming her and talking in a soothing voice. He watched her for a minute before Scarlett snorted.

Diana glanced up and said, "It's okay, girl," then kept brushing. "What brings you out here this morning, Andy?"

"Diana, when you were a kid and Dad and I had you thrown out that horrible night..."

Her hand froze, and she shot him a quick glance, filled with so much pain and anger, before she glanced down. For a minute, he was positive her hand trembled.

"I'm sorry, Diana, for what I did. You never deserved to be treated that way. But I need to know this: When we tossed Faye, you, and your sister out that night and burned your house, how did you survive? I mean, look what you've done with yourself. You're respectable. You didn't become your mother."

Diana sighed and rested her brush on Scarlett, looking away. "That was a really hard time, Andy. I suppose I still carry it with me. I was always respectable, you just didn't see it, and neither did the townspeople. I was judged for my mother's sins, if you recall. I was just a kid trying to hold together a whole family, and I prayed every night that everyone would see me for who I really was inside. I even prayed for you to really see me, to love me. I just wanted the one thing we all want: love. I was young and foolish, Andy. Oh, I look back now and see it had to happen to get me here. But the end doesn't justify the means." She unlatched the gate and slipped out, sliding the lock back in place.

Andy watched her now. Just being around her, he sensed that she oozed with passion, beauty that made him want to spend every moment with her. How he envied Jed. He looked away first to break the spell. She was his cousin's wife, and he realized now that he'd always love her. What had then made sense didn't now.

"Jed's a lucky man, Diana."

She tossed the brush into the box on the floor and wiped her hands. "And I'm a lucky woman to have found Jed."

He cleared his throat before they went any further down that road, the one that was best left buried. "We may have a problem." Andy quickly explained his visit to his lawyer and what Clint had said about Laura. He hesitated but then decided to share his worries of his mother's involvement.

Diana listened and nodded, but she grew quiet when she was thinking, and she frowned. She reached out and touched Andy's arm, patting it, and said, "I need to go get changed and take Laura to see her son. But thank you. I already suspected we'd have trouble convincing the court that Laura would be able to support her son, get them a home of their own. Your mother, though, that makes me nervous, Andy." She started to walk away and then turned back. "Would you be willing to testify on Laura's behalf of her mistreatment and vouch for her character?"

"Of course I will. And Diana, would you mind if I came along with you and Laura to see her son?" Andy thought Diana had the most brilliant blue eyes, and with her deep red hair pinned up in a haphazard bun and dirt streaking her cheek, he had to swallow to think clearly. "I'd like to be there to support Laura in some way. I can only imagine how tough it will be for her."

"It's going to be really emotional, Andy. Laura's going to be a mess, and her son... I don't know what to say about him. But maybe it might help, having you there."

He gazed over her head when Laura stepped out of the house.

Diana touched his arm. "I'll go get cleaned up." She turned and jogged toward the house, calling out to Jed before hurrying inside.

Jed followed her in, leaving Laura outside. Andy took a deep breath before taking his first step over to Laura.

CHAPTER 18

The drive to the foster parents' house took almost half an hour. They lived on a rural acreage, the forest and mountains majestically set in the background. The weather, though, wasn't as pleasant. The rain and wind had kicked up, pounding the windshield, and the temperature was dropping so low that the rain most likely would turn to snow before the day was out. So, of course, Jed jumped in, and he, too, insisted that Andy drive.

Andy had held the seat back for Diana, and she said as she climbed in, "Jed doesn't like me driving if it rains, snows, just about any time the road conditions are questionable. So I expected Andy to drive, or else Jed would be driving us over himself, Laura."

Laura had just taken that in, absorbing how a husband could love his wife so much that he'd worry when she drove. Wow, it was a dream, and she was envious of Diana and what she had with Jed. Jed made her nervous, but most men did. He was so strong, tall, and solidly built, and she never knew what to say around him. But she realized that Jed wasn't a talker; he studied people and seemed to figure them out by watching. But then, Laura wasn't much of a talker either. The problem was that when the two of them were put together, the silence could become awkward.

Andy, though, was a mystery to her. He made her nervous. He oozed power, everything alpha, and she was baffled as to why he wanted to help her. Oh, she got the part where he felt responsible, but he was going above and beyond, and that made her ridiculously nervous. No one ever went out of their way for Laura. Even with Diana, helping as she did, Laura kept half expecting to wake up to Diana telling her she had changed her mind, that she had to leave, that her problems were too much. But she hadn't said squat along those lines, and neither had Andy.

Diana and Andy chatted. She knew that every time Andy took his eyes off the road and glanced her way, she could feel his concern, his caring, and she didn't know what to make of it. He was, after all, far too attractive for his own good. The truth was that he made her nervous not because he watched her in a way that was inappropriate but because she had watched him in the same way. Every time he walked into a room in the estate, she'd hidden behind a potted plant, a door, anything for him not to see her, to notice her.

Laura pulled herself from her thoughts when Andy turned down a gravel road with trees lining both sides. He drove to the end and braked. "This the address, 3620, Diana?"

Diana leaned over the seat. "Good eye, Andy. I never would have seen it through all those overgrown bushes."

Andy turned down a narrow dirt driveway. A rotted sign with the house address was painted onto a board as if a five-year-old had done it. The broken board was tilted sideways. The driveway angled around and opened into a cleared-out dirt yard, with broken-down cars piled every-where, a chicken coop that had seen better days, several old buildings, and a two-story house that didn't appear finished. The outside was covered in tar paper, and piles of lumber and garbage were stacked beside the house. Andy parked behind what appeared to be half a dozen vehicles. Laura gazed at the porch, which had a punching bag hung by chains and an old sofa with a big dog lying on it.

"Diana, is this where my son is?" Her voice sounded weak. When she looked over, she didn't miss the hard set of Andy's jaw.

He nodded his head. "I'll go check it out, and you two wait here."

"Andy, wait…" Diana started to protest, but he'd already jumped out and shut the door. He stepped up on the porch, which was missing a front step, and pounded on the door.

Laura turned as Diana climbed over the front seat and sat in the driver's side. "The Friessen men, in case you didn't notice, Laura, don't ever sit back and let anyone take charge, let alone a woman." Diana yanked open the door. "Let's go. Looks like someone answered the door."

Diana walked with Laura. Andy was speaking with a short, plump woman who appeared to be in her fifties. There was a small dog barking and barking, which she bent over to pick up. A cat ran out the door and scurried around the house. Andy glanced down at Laura when she approached. The light-haired woman holding the yapping dog turned her head and yelled, "Nancy, turn that down!" She was yelling at someone upstairs. Then the volume on what Laura thought was the TV lowered. The woman returned to the open door. "Which one of you is the mother?"

Laura felt stung, but it was Andy who spoke. "This is

Laura Parnell. She is Gabriel's mother." Andy touched her shoulder, and she didn't flinch. With the way the woman stared at her with hard judgmental eyes, she welcomed his support. Her heart was pounding, she was terrified, and her heart ached to see her child.

"Well, come in. It's cold out there." The hallway wasn't even finished. The floor was plywood with an old rug thrown over it, and the walls were gyprock. She led them up a steep stairwell, with no handrail, which was open to downstairs.

Andy led the way into a large, open living room, kitchen, and dining area. The dining room wall had insulation covered by a plastic vapor barrier. The ceiling had the same, and the walls were unfinished. Two dressers were pressed against the wall in the overcrowded living room. The television was on, and there were five young children sitting on the floor, watching it. The woman carried that yappy dog that continued to bark. Laura looked around frantically but didn't see Gabriel with the other children.

"Andy, where's Gabriel?"

The way the woman watched her, she didn't want to talk to her. Andy didn't appear too happy as he looked around this house, if it could be called a house, that was. She had seen his darker moods and recognized one now.

"Where is Gabriel?" he asked, staring down at the woman, his arms crossed.

The woman had soft brown eyes that widened as she spoke. "Oh, he's in the bedroom. I'll get him." There were what appeared to be two bedrooms off this square room and another door that was closed. A toilet flushed behind that one. The room the woman went to had a half door with a bolt, similar to something used on stall doors. She slid the bolt open and went in. Diana followed the woman and looked in, but Laura couldn't get her feet to move. Her little boy, Gabriel, came out holding the woman's other hand. She still held the yappy dog. Gabriel saw her and raced to her, and Laura went down on her knees and crushed him in a tight hug, struggling to hold back her tears.

They stayed for only an hour. Andy lingered in the background. She could feel him watching over them, and again she was so glad he was there. The woman, though, watched Laura the entire time, and after an hour stood up and said, "You're done, time to go. Say goodbye." Then the women said to Andy, "I don't want a scene, or the boy upset or the other kids. I don't need to be calming them down all night." It was Andy who got Laura through it, who leaned down and wrapped his arms around her when they both sobbed, and he whispered in her ear, "I'm going to get him back for you, I promise." When Laura stood up with Andy's help, Gabriel reached for her, screaming, but the woman yelled. "Get out now! I told you not to upset him." She grabbed Gabriel and took him back in the room, shutting the door while they left.

Laura didn't know how she had gotten into the car, but Andy buckled her seatbelt and was holding her hand as they drove away. Diana sat quietly in back.

CHAPTER 19

Andy was dressed in a dark green suit, one of many he'd had custom tailored earlier this year. He looked the part, like a wealthy millionaire, as he strode into the virtually empty Arlington courtroom where Diana, Jed, and Laura waited. He didn't have any time to meet with Diana or speak with Jed before the courtroom doors closed and the other witnesses entered: the counsel for Child Protective Services, the deputy, the sheriff, and an overweight man Andy presumed to be the social worker who had taken Gabriel away, based on how Laura stiffened when she saw him.

A clerk announced the judge and the case. Laura moved beside Diana at the defense table and glanced back at Andy. He reached forward and rubbed Laura's back, and she smiled for the first time at him. Diana glanced at the closed door and then at Andy. She leaned over the rail and whispered, "Where's Stan?"

Andy shook his head as an awful feeling cranked up the anxiety he already felt whispering like a tornado behind him. Stan headed up family law and worked for Clint at his family's law firm. He couldn't help but suspect his mother's hand in this, but after the horrifying day yesterday, when he'd taken Laura to visit her son, he was consumed by how Gabriel could have been put in such an unsuitable place. He was pretty sure he had been locked in that room, and the other kids who stared blankly at the television had been ripped away from their parents, too. The house itself wasn't liveable, so how in God's name were those people suitable foster parents? This made absolutely no sense. He'd talked briefly with Diana after they'd returned to the ranch. She, too, had been horrified, as she'd grown up in a foster home that was loving and decent, with an older couple who'd later adopted her. Andy had tossed and turned all night and even ignored his mother's rant that morning before he slipped out the back door. His father followed him outside and demanded he stop this nonsense with "that girl, the maid" and get back inside to repair the damage with Alexis, or Jed would end up paying the consequences.

He'd hesitated, but the screams that haunted him from the past were enough to have him get in his truck and drive away. He could not—would not—stand for another child to ever suffer that way again. Now, as he stared back at Diana and shook his head, he understood what it meant to be at the mercy of someone powerful. "Can you do this without him?" Andy whispered.

She looked at Jed and nodded. "I'll do my best."

The judge sat and cracked his gavel, drawing everyone's attention. He was an older, graying man with thick glasses. He read a file and then peered up at Laura. "So, are you the young mother who was sleeping in a car with your son?"

Laura glanced at Diana; Diana gripped her hand before she could speak.

"Your honor, this is my client, Laura Parnell..."

The judge snapped and jabbed a stubby finger at Laura. "I asked this young lady, so you will please be quiet."

Andy glanced at Jed. Diana appeared to visibly start. "Your honor, this is highly inappropriate. I am the counsel for Laura and am here to speak for her."

The judge snapped and appeared angry. "Miss, you will speak when I tell you to. Is that understood? This is my courtroom, my rules."

Andy watched, wondering for a moment if there was a camera planted somewhere and if someone would jump out at any moment and say, "The joke's on you!" Laura appeared completely confused. Diana patted her hand and whispered something in her ear.

"Yes, Your Honor, I had my son, Gabriel, with me in the car. But it was only for the night. I have a job now...."

The judge snapped again. "What you did was reckless endangerment of a child, out in the cold, your child hungry. I know there are some judges who lean toward giving parents' chances at the expense of a child's welfare, which is completely against the principles of protecting a child. Where is your husband during this, anyway?" The judge glared at Laura, and Andy wanted to push through the gate and stand beside her.

But Diana cleared her throat. "Your Honor..."

"I did not ask you to speak. You, speak. You, be quiet." He jabbed his finger again toward Laura, then Diana. Diana glanced back at Jed and Andy, her face pale, her eyes snapping with fire.

Laura's face was tinged pink, and Diana wrote something down on a pad of paper and gestured to it. Laura stuttered, "Your Honor, I'm not married."

"Now, why doesn't that surprise me?" the judge growled. "Fine, let's move on. Mister Tate, is it?"

The counsel for Child Services slid back his chair and stood slowly, buttoning his gray blazer. He wore round glasses, and his blond hair was in a stylishly short cut. "Yes, Your Honor, I'm the counsel for Child Services. We ask that you deny the petition until a thorough investigation can be conducted. The mother was found in a dilapidated old car parked at a shopping mall overnight, where loitering is strictly prohibited, with her child. It rained, and the temperature dropped to thirty degrees overnight. The deputy who discovered them reported that they were both cold and the child appeared hungry. With the mandate of Child Protective Services, in cases where we see an imminent danger to a child, immediate apprehension is warranted. The sheriff acted, and the said child, Gabriel Parnell, is now in the care of the state. We'd also note to the court that there appears to be a neurological deficit with the said minor and would ask the court's permission to have him assessed."

Laura grabbed Diana's arm and whispered angrily.

Diana jumped up. "I object, Your Honor. Neurological deficit? What is this? I think the mother here has the right to know what is going on."

Andy nudged Jed. He shook his head, and by the way his cheek twitched, Andy knew he was furious with what was going on here, most likely with how the judge was talking to his wife.

"Miss... what is your name?" the judge asked in a way that made it sound as if Diana were wasting everyone's time.

"That's Missus Friessen, sir." She ground the words out.

The judge jerked off his glasses and squinted, sitting up straighter. It was obvious to this judge that the Friessen name meant something. The judge gestured toward Mr.

Tate. "I have to agree with Missus Friessen. What is this neurological deficit? Come on. Details, please." The judge gestured toward the counsel.

Mr. Tate glanced back at the social worker and whispered something. The social worker stood.

"Your Honor, I would ask that Hank Walker, the social worker who apprehended the minor, be allowed to speak, as he has details on the problem that's been brought to light."

"Of course. Mister Walker, step forward," responded the judge.

Hank Walker pushed the gate open. He was a man of average height and a large girth, wearing a ratty tweed jacket and a green, spotted tie. He swept back his brown hair, which was a little on the long side and drooped over his forehead. "Your Honor, Gabriel Parnell is unable to talk. He is a four-year-old boy. He has loud outbursts and screaming fits and doesn't appear to understand when the foster parents he's been placed with communicate with him. These parents have been in the foster system for twenty years, taking in hundreds of children who've needed a home, many emergency situations like this. Child development comes naturally, and they've had more than their share of special needs children. Fetal Alcohol Syndrome tops the list. So the basic medical needs of this child, as well, have been overlooked. I mean, your honor, they suspect there is something wrong with this child. He may need medication It's a serious problem, and the generous folks fostering this boy need to be granted the authority to have him assessed." Hank glanced at Mr. Tate.

The judge cleared his throat. "Mister Walker, thank you for clarifying this. I think I'm ready to rule."

Diana jumped up again, and Andy was ready to push

through the gate. "Your Honor, you have not allowed our petition to be heard, and we have witnesses to call. These so-called foster parents..."

The judge waved his pudgy hand. "Next outburst from you and I'll hold you in contempt, and you'll be spending the night as a guest of the county jail. Now sit down. I'm ready to rule."

The judge cleared his throat and appeared to be reading something. "There is evidence of gross negligence on the part of the young mother, part of which I contribute to age, to being too young to have the wisdom to raise a child. With no father in the picture and the addition of the gross neglect of an obvious medical problem, maybe from the mother drinking while pregnant, she has added another FAS child to society, another tax payers' burden."

Laura gasped. Diana grabbed her arm and shook her head.

The judge glanced angrily at Laura. "Gabriel will stay a ward of the state, and I grant the state the right to assume and take care of all medical needs of the child, so yes, by all means, get this child assessed or whatever it is you need to do, Mister Walker. And until such assessment takes place, the mother shall be limited to supervised visits, which she will arrange through Mister Walker after the New Year. The visits will last no more than one hour and will be supervised by a state social worker." The judge cracked his gavel and pushed his bulky frame from the chair, exiting the courtroom.

"What the hell was that?" Andy leaned across the rail and glanced back at Jed, who was shaking his head, and then to Diana, who stuffed papers in her briefcase. Laura didn't move. She sat frozen in the hard wooden chair, staring straight ahead.

"I'd say we were just ambushed," Diana snapped, and then she dropped her briefcase and faced Jed and Andy, raising both hands as she shut her eyes tight for a second, as if she needed to compose herself. "I've never seen anything like this. This was a Mickey Mouse show. That wasn't justice. That was something planned, rehearsed. Did you see that the judge only listened when I said my name was Missus Friessen? He paused and appeared startled. So what do you think is up with that?"

"Andy, what about that fancy lawyer of yours that was supposed to be here?" Jed barked in a low growl.

But it was Diana who answered: "I'd say they planned to leave me high and dry. What are the chances your mother's hand is in this, Andy?"

"I never drank when I was pregnant. Why would he say that?" Laura never turned around when she spoke, her voice barely a whisper. This time, Andy did push through the gate and walked around the table to Laura. Her face was pasty white, and her eyes were red rimmed.

Diana said, "Laura, that wasn't what the social worker said, and as far as the judge saying that, well, he was out of line. A superior court would overrule this. Laura, we're going to get an apology. But I've got to tell you, with the healthcare crisis in this country, with so many who still can't afford health insurance, it made absolutely no sense that they said you denied your child medical care. I'm speechless." Diana patted Laura's shoulder.

Laura didn't move. Her shoulders were hunched forward, and a tear fell down her cheek. "But it's Christmas, and they took my child away. I can't even see him again before Christmas, he said. He won't be home for Christmas, not that I have a home, anyway."

"Diana, what now?" Andy asked. For the first time ever,

he felt helpless, and he was pretty sure his mother had been responsible for this.

She shook her head. "We need to go. I'm going to call a colleague in Seattle, get some help." The social worker and counsel left the courtroom with the sheriff and deputy, without saying a word to Diana. "Let's go," she said.

It was Andy who helped Laura up, and Diana led the way out. Andy helped Laura into the backseat of the SUV, while Diana climbed in front. He held Laura's hand for a second, and she looked at him, the light gone from her eyes, and said, "Thank you, Andy. Thank you for helping me."

Andy didn't know what to say, but he skimmed her cheek where a tear fell and used his thumb to wipe it away. "We'll get him back."

Jed touched his shoulder and leaned in, glancing at Laura. "Andy, are you coming out to the ranch? There isn't much you can do right now."

Laura still held his hand.

"Actually, I think there is." Andy squeezed Laura's hand and pulled away when he realized then what he needed to do.

"Oh, do you care to fill me in?" Jed asked.

"I'll call you later." Andy waved as he hurried to his truck, yanking open the door and sliding behind the wheel, wondering how one prepared before marching in to deal with the devil.

CHAPTER 20

"Mother!" Andy shouted as he slammed the front door and strode across the grand entryway.

Jules, of course, came running. "Sir, please, is there something you need?"

"Where's Mother?"

"I'm right here," Caroline called to him from the library.

When he strode in, she was sitting behind his desk, dressed in a dark blue silk pantsuit. She had his drawers open and was sifting through his personal records, which had been in a locked drawer.

"What the hell are you doing in my desk?"

She leaned back and crossed her legs, clasping her hands. "How was your morning, Andy?"

The way she said it, Andy knew she had been responsible for that circus in the courtroom. His mother had connections, money, but he never thought she had this kind of power. He obviously didn't know her very well, and that terrified him. "Why would you do that to Laura? What did she ever do to you? You had your temper tantrum. Her child was taken away, for God's sake. What kind of monster are you?"

"Andy, sit down, and don't talk to your mother that way." Todd Friessen was lounging on the sofa—Andy hadn't seen him sitting there when he walked in.

"What the hell is this? Dad, we were always close, but doing this to an innocent girl is not okay. Which one of you was responsible for that carnival at court this morning?" Andy didn't move but stepped back to really see both his parents. Right now, he didn't like this vision of the two of them allied together. He wished for a moment that his father would take off with a new mistress, leave town for a while.

"That was necessary. We warned you, and apparently the threat to have your cousin's funding pulled wasn't enough incentive for you. After that stunt last night with Alexis, you humiliated her, abandoning her like that right before dinner. She couldn't face anyone for dinner; she was to be seated beside you. Can you imagine the humiliation for her, seeing your name on the place setting but being greeted by an empty chair? There were whispers, but fortunately for you, it was hinted that you were so crazy about Alexis that you two snuck off together. The senator knew the truth, and he's still livid. So you have a choice, Anderson: You will either knock off this foolishness and get to know Alexis or you'll be responsible for a whole lot of misery. I think a spring wedding would be best." Caroline spoke as if this were just a casual business deal.

"I don't think so. I made it clear to you before that you will never have any say in who and when I marry!" Andy shouted.

Todd laughed. "Actually, son, it's your choice. You see, Laura Parnell will never see her child again unless you make this happen. And remember, too, it's amazing the things that turn up in people's pasts. Dear, weren't you telling me that several pieces of your jewelry are missing, and they were last seen before Laura cleaned your room? How many days ago was that? And Jed, wow, do you remember that incident Jed had with his brothers when they were teens, the time the sheriff brought them home with... what was it, theft, vandalism, public mischief? I guess the details don't really matter. We just need to allude to the crime—they can dig and find out what really happened. Oh, that's right. The senator doesn't like any hint of a scandal, so by the time Jed straightens it out, his funding will be gone for good."

Andy felt ice water chill his blood. He shut his eyes and started to leave, but then he stopped. He'd seen firsthand today just how far his parents were willing to go, so whatever deal they had with the senator, they needed him to make it happen. "So if things go your way, will Laura get her son back?"

"Well, it's getting awfully close to Christmas, so can we expect your answer tonight?" Caroline asked.

Andy only nodded and left, fearing what he needed to do for a young lady named Laura who was out of her league, a pawn in a dirty game she had never signed on for.

CHAPTER 21

Andy had shed his jacket and tie. There was a misty rain falling, and the daylight was fading from the gray skies as he leaned against his bedroom window. The night was turning colder, and Andy couldn't fathom how Laura had spent two nights in her car. She still didn't have a home. Jed and Diana couldn't let her stay forever. They didn't have room, and those cabins beside the house still hadn't been winterized and were only used in the summer months when booked by the summer riders that Jed took out on pack trips.

A soft knock on his door pulled him from his thoughts. "Come in," he shouted.

He didn't look to see who was there, but he sensed her, smelled her as she approached.

"You ran out on me."

"I'm sorry. I didn't mean to embarrass you." Andy lifted a lock of her silky brown hair.

She just stared at him with an innocence he'd never seen before. She gazed at his lips, and Andy touched her cheek with the back of his fingers. She turned her head inward and pressed her lips to his fingers. Andy bent his head, and her mouth opened under the force of his. His tongue moved in, touching hers.

Alexis buried her fingers in his hair, dug her nails into his skull. Andy walked her back to the bed and lowered her. She wrapped her arms around his thickly muscled shoulders and hugged him even closer to her. The slow movements of her hips beneath him urged him on. He reached behind her and slid the zipper down her dress, sliding his hand and pulling the straps down, exposing a barely decent black lace bra. She was stunning as he ran his hand over her generous breasts and then froze, rolling off her to the side and resting his arm across his forehead. He could feel the way she stiffened and could hear her turn away and pull her dress up.

"Alexis, I'm so sorry. Embarrassing you is not what I want to do. But I can't do this. I can't be forced to make love to you, to marry you. The woman I marry, I need to love with my whole heart. You deserve better."

She didn't look at him but kept her back to him as she slid off the bed in the dim room, reaching for the zipper he'd lowered. "Then why would you pretend? I don't deserve that."

Andy sat up on the edge of the bed. "Alexis, this is about a young lady named Laura. She was fired by my mother just before you arrived for accidentally knocking over a Christmas tree. She had a little boy, four years old. She's twenty, got pregnant at fifteen, and her parents threw her out. She worked to support her kid, put a roof over their head, to feed them, and she was barely getting by when my mother had her escorted off the property without her pitiful pay. She couldn't pay rent, buy food, and she was thrown out of her home by her predator of a landlord. She was forced to sleep in her car with her son and was begging for a job. She was found by a deputy one night, and he had her child taken away, ripped right from her arms. Can you imagine a woman who loved her child so much she'd do everything to protect him? Then, for me to discover my mother's hand in keeping a child from his mother in court today…"

Alexis stood with her back to him, her hand on the door handle. Slowly, she turned. Her eyes flashed with anger. "Your mother is keeping a child from his mother?" She took a step away from the door and placed her hands on her shapely, very sexy hips. "Sounds to me like what you need is a wife."

CHAPTER 22

Andy drove down the long driveway, lit up on each side by white, green, and red lights, and parked at the front doors of the estate. The round, circular driveway was normally used by guests—the family always parked in back. Christmas lights blinked in a rainbow of colors, strewn on the trees in front of the estate and strung across the roofline of the house. He shut off the engine and stepped out, wearing his dark suit. He walked around to the passenger side and opened her door, holding out his hand. She hesitated before slipping her slender, pale hand in his. Her white gown slid up, exposing slim, shapely legs, and she stepped down in gold-trimmed high-heeled sandals.

A slim gold band glittered from her ring finger. It wasn't something he'd ever considered buying. He'd always expected to buy his wife a big diamond, maybe a pear-shaped emerald, something that made a statement. Andy wore no ring himself as he held his wife's hand. She paused at the bottom of the wide stone steps, and when he felt her trembling, he realized she was frightened. He ran his hand over her long, silky hair. "Let's go in. Don't worry. Every-thing's going to be okay."

She hesitated and searched out his gaze before nodding. He slid his arm around her shoulders as they walked up the stairs together. When he opened the front door, they heard voices chattering from the guests who lingered in the grand foyer. There appeared to be a hundred people here. "Wait here," he said, and he climbed the stairs until he looked down on the crowd and shouted, "Could I have your atten-tion, please?" He stuck two fingers in his mouth and whis-tled until the room fell quiet. His mother and father pushed through the crowd and peered up at him, and he could see the concern and worry in their expressions. But then, of course his mother quickly smiled to her friends and the people around her. "Can I have your attention, please? I have an announcement to make."

Alexis moved to the bottom of the stairs and smiled up at him.

"I'd like to add to this celebration by introducing you all to my bride."

Cheers and whistles echoed from the crowd, and his mother smiled and clapped, glancing at Alexis.

Andy extended his hand out. "My wife, Missus Laura Friessen. Come on up here, darling."

His mother gasped her eyes flashing with anger before she quickly hid it. Laura lifted the white gown Diana had snared from a boutique in the mall. It was a simple white gown, not a wedding dress, with small capped sleeves and a v-cut in the front, and she strode up the dozen stairs to where her husband waited. She put her hand in his. He pulled her to his side and leaned down, kissing her long enough that the crowd cheered. He sensed her innocence, her inexperience, from her trembling lips. When he pulled away, she blushed brightly. Alexis raised her glass at the bottom of the stairs and strode to his mother, to Todd, to where the senator was glaring at Andy as if he'd just yanked the rug out from under him.

"I'd like to propose a toast," Alexis said. "Please, everyone, raise your glasses. To my good friend Andy Friessen and his lovely wife, Laura. Please, everyone, help wish them a joyous and blissfully happy marriage filled with love and lots of children, and to Laura's little boy, Gabriel, who will be arriving here tomorrow morning. Isn't that right, Father, Caroline?" Alexis allowed her gaze to linger on Todd, Caroline, and then her father. Then she raised her glass to them and winked.

Everyone cheered and drank.

"Come on." Andy took Laura's hand and led her back down the stairs, where they were surrounded by well-wishers and made their way through the crowd to Alexis. She stood with his parents and the senator, who all masked their rage with plastic smiles they'd mastered years ago. Caroline accepted hugs from several friends, who squealed their excitement.

Alexis set her glass on the tray of a passing waiter. "I'll be leaving in the morning, Father, Caroline, Todd, but I'd like to thank you for your hospitality and the enlightening stay. I'm sure you'll have no trouble seeing that Laura's son arrives safely tomorrow, which is Christmas Eve."

Caroline flashed an icy smile, showing all of her perfectly straight teeth, nodding at friends who waved across the room. "Why, you little bitch."

"Don't ever talk to my daughter like that," the senator snapped. He stepped closer, leaning in. "Alexis, I'd like to speak with you in private."

"While you're at it, tell her that Laura has just lost her

child for good," Caroline muttered, so low that no one would overhear.

Alexis chuckled softly under her breath. "You may want to rethink that, since your little offshore partnership and the investments that will net you billions might come crashing down around you. With the recent election, it's frowned on when billionaires and senators are partnering up to take jobs from those in their own state, their own country, and ship them overseas. And with all the subsidies you've managed to streamline your way... this will make a great story, especially from a senator's daughter."

The senator reached for her arm and smiled, but his eyes flashed with a glimpse of the predator he'd always kept from her. "Are you blackmailing your own father?"

"Yes. When a senator abuses his power with a wealthy woman to destroy an impoverished single mother, to separate her from her child, that's where I draw the line, Daddy. I love you, but I'm ashamed to know you right now." She didn't move but glared at his hand until he dropped it from her arm.

"It's not that easy to get her child back. For God's sake, it's Christmas Eve tomorrow. It can't be done," the senator whispered.

Alexis patted his hand, glancing at Caroline and Todd as she spoke. "You'll find a way to make it happen. I have faith in you, all of you. You're a great team when you want to be." She turned when she glimpsed Andy, with Laura in tow, making his way toward her. "Excuse me. I need to congratulate the bride and groom. Oh, and Caroline, I expect that you'll welcome her into your family."

Caroline's smile faltered, and she pushed through the crowd, excusing herself. Todd stood with the senator when Andy approached.

"Dad, Senator, I'd like you to meet my wife, Laura." Andy wrapped his arm around Laura's trembling shoulder, and he pulled her closer when Todd reached for her hand and kissed it. She yanked it away, and Todd's expression darkened right before he strode off.

The senator's face was a stony mask. "If you'll excuse me, I have a call to make."

Alexis stepped in and hugged Andy. He held her and then kissed her cheek. "How can I ever thank you? What you did... Alexis, I'm sorry. I never expected you to help the way you did. You're a true angel."

She patted his arm and then reached out and touched Laura, who was standing off to the side awkwardly. "A mother and child should never be separated," she said.

When Alexis glanced at Andy, he saw something in that one look that resembled a profound sadness. Then it was gone. This time, when she looked at Laura and Andy, she smiled.

"You two look great together. And don't you worry, Laura. Your son will be home tomorrow. But I have a plane to catch in the morning, so if you'll excuse me, I need to go pack."

Laura stopped her just as she tried to squeeze past. "Alexis, I've never had anyone do anything to help me, not like this. I don't know why you did it. But thank you."

Alexis patted her shoulder and made her way to the stairs, which she hurried up, lifting her dark skirt.

"Come on, I know you're hungry. Let's grab something to eat." Andy held Laura's hand, guiding her to the dining room, where food covered the table. He glanced at her face and watched the wonder and astonishment as she widened her eyes.

"That's a lot of food, Andy. That will feed a lot of people."

"Yes, it will." Andy reached for a plate and dished up food for Laura and then for himself and found them a quiet spot off the sunroom to eat in peace. The party was still in full swing when Andy led her upstairs to his room. He closed the door, and she hesitated just inside the bedroom. When she looked up at him, it wasn't fear that he saw, but innocence. He strode toward her and slid his hands down her side, and then he led her into his large en suite.

"I want you to relax. Have a bath. There's a nightgown for you to put on—I asked Jules to find it." He gestured to the stacked fresh towels and a plain white nightgown, and then he left, pulling the door closed behind him.

Half an hour later, she opened the door and walked sheepishly out, holding her hands in front of the fabric. She glanced at the bed and blushed. "Which side would you like?"

"The left," he said, and he watched her walk around and slip under the duvet, pulling it up to her chin. He smiled to himself. Of all the women he'd had, he had never in a million years imagined himself with someone this inexperienced.

Andy undressed and slipped in under the sheet. He moved on his side and hooked an arm around her waist to pull her firmly back into the cradle of his body. He felt her tension ease when she touched his hand, which rested on her stomach over her nightgown. She was hesitant at first, touching his hand and then resting it on top of hers. He didn't push, just let her settle.

"This is really nice."

"Go to sleep," he said, feeling the tension build inside himself, and he thought he would go half blind lying there with her pressed into him. Never once had he lain with a woman all night without satisfying his needs. Just what the hell had he been thinking? God knew he would have loved to roll her over onto her back to seduce her, to feel her warmth. He could do it easily, but he wanted the decision made by her consciously, not because he knew how to stoke her fire, how to get her so hot she'd easily allow him his way.

She turned to face him. "When you showed up at Diana and Jed's and asked me to marry you, I thought you were joking. Then I thought it was pity, and I did it to get Gabriel back. But I don't want to be a burden. Or the other woman. I can't be that."

He touched her lips with his, a slow, deep kiss. She touched his shoulders as he slid his hand down her stomach, to her hip and her thigh. She sighed, and he deepened the kiss as he slid up her nightgown and caressed her bare buttocks. She moaned and pressed her bottom against his hand. He couldn't wait much longer, and he suspected she knew that. He rolled her over onto her back, resting above her on his forearms. "This will be a real marriage, and you'll be the only woman."

He watched her in the dim room. The only light was from the Christmas lights decorating the house and lighting up the property, all shining in from the windows as he had left the curtains wide open. He'd done it for a reason, because he wanted to see her, all of her, even though, as he watched her now, a slight blush crept up her cheeks. She was so young and innocent even though she had a child, and he could sense all of that in her hesitation.

"I don't want to disappoint you." She slid her hand so cautiously, so slowly to his cheek and touched him.

He leaned in and tasted her again, and she opened for

him, touching her tongue with his as he deepened the kiss. Sliding his hand down her side to lift both ends of the nightgown and pull it over her head, he tossed it on the floor. He gazed at her full breasts that fit nicely in the palm of his hands, her slim hips and flat tummy, she almost seemed too thin, but Andy had every intention of changing that as he ran his hand over her stomach, the covers pulled down and moved to her side. She reached for him, pulling his head toward her, and he knew he wouldn't last when she slid her hand down his chest and lower to take him in her hand.

"No, Laura." He chuckled when he sensed her hesitation, as if she'd done something she shouldn't.

"I'm sorry..." she said, and he could hear how nervous she was.

"Don't be sorry. I just won't last if you touch me." He watched her blink then, her seductive green eyes widening. If she ever learned how to use her sexuality on him, he'd be in big trouble. Then it dawned on her, his meaning, as her eyes widened more, and before she could think it to death and pull back, he leaned in and kissed her again, tasting her until she started to relax beside him. He took her nipple in his mouth and slid his hand over her other breast, squeezing and touching her lower until she moaned in his mouth, and he moved over her, on top of her, spreading her thighs, feeling how ready she was, and he watched her as he slowly filled her and she gasped. He whispered, "Easy, baby," and held himself still, starting to ease out as it may have been too much too fast, but she slid her hands over his ass and pulled him back.

"No, don't pull out. You feel so good." She slid her hand, her arms, around his back, ran her hands over his shoulders as he moved inside her, doing his damnedest to take it slow and easy. She wrapped her legs around his waist, and he could feel her coming apart beneath him, whispering his name over and over, and Andy couldn't hold back any longer.

LAURA NEVER DREAMED she'd have a husband, let alone a man who looked at her the way Andy Friessen had. As he lay beside her now, and she listened to his heavy breathing, she could still feel every touch, every caress, where he had touched and tasted every part of her as she lay nestled in his arms. For the first time, she felt hope, love, something she had never dreamed. With each touch, he had taught her what it was like to be a woman. With each kiss, he had her feeling things she had never thought possible, and when she took him in her body, he completed her. Now, as he held her in the dark, she knew Andy Friessen would do anything for her.

CHAPTER 23

"We never finished any formal assessment, but here's the preliminary information from a pediatrician who assessed Gabriel. He lists it all in there, but basically he notes a serious developmental delay, an inability to establish and maintain relationships with his peers, a serious delay in language development. He plays by himself, gets agitated, and screams in fits, and his foster parents were unable to comfort him. We can only assume how long the mother's ignored this." Hank Walker, the social worker, handed the manila envelope to Andy.

"You take a child away from his mother and stick him with a bunch of strangers in some shack that's barely livable, with how many other kids in the system, locking him in a bedroom—all that behavior sounds pretty normal to me." Andy was barely able to control his rage, but he didn't much like how the social worker alluded to Laura being an unfit mother. It was unfair what had been said about her. She did the best she could, and she loved Gabriel. "Maybe you should ask yourself how and where a single mother who struggles to feed her kid, to shelter her child, and then work herself to the bone is going to afford any medical help—let alone get it. She didn't have your resources, but you can bet she now has mine. I'll make damn sure both Gabriel and Laura are taken care of. But, Mister Walker, please don't ever make the mistake of judging my wife again. She is my wife, and you will treat her with respect."

The man had the good grace to flush, at least, but he didn't say a word as he turned away and left. Andy shut the front door and pressed his hand against it, taking a deep breath to calm down. The fact was he couldn't stand that guy, the social worker. The prick had treated Laura as if she was a nobody, but the only crimes she had were being poor and getting pregnant at fifteen.

Andy pushed away from the door and started toward the library to join his wife and Gabriel, but he stopped when he spotted Aida standing outside the room, smiling at Laura, who was on her knees beside the Christmas tree with Gabriel beside her, playing with the train that circled the track. Gabriel stared at the mountains of gifts wrapped with shiny bows and paper that glittered. Andy moved beside Aida, and when she gazed up at him, there were tears in her eyes. For the first time ever, she smiled at him, showing her crooked teeth, and then patted his arm with her bony, wrinkled hand. "Merry Christmas, Andy, and bless you and your family. You did right by her. Didn't expect you to marry her. Never saw that one coming, Andy. First time in a long time someone surprised me as you did." Aida shook her head. "You brought a mother and child together. You take care of her and Gabriel."

"I will, Aida. I do care for her." He didn't look at Aida when he said it but felt his heart leap when Laura glanced up and met his gaze from across the room in a private moment that was theirs alone, a glimmer of peace and hope in her eyes.

"Oh, I think you more than care for her. Her, too. Love lives there. You need a chance to get to know each other." She patted his chest where his heart was. "You may not realize it yet, but you're building something deep and meaningful that will last a lifetime. It can be really good if you let it." The old cook's expression changed, and she nodded as if holding back a tide of emotions, then walked away.

"Merry Christmas, Aida, and thank you," Andy called out.

She paused for a second and glanced over her shoulder, giving him an amused smile. "There's hope for you yet, Andy Friessen," she said, and then she retreated into the kitchen.

Andy joined his wife and stepson on the floor beside the tree, watching the toy train zoom around the track. He slid his arm around Laura's waist, and she leaned back into him, and he kissed the top of her head. She smiled up at him with those glimmering green eyes, and Gabriel reached out and touched Andy's hand, grinning with innocence and such love. Andy ran his hand over Gabriel's dark hair and over his shoulder as the innocent little boy's smile reached out to him, as if Andy were his hero and somehow Gabriel knew that Andy would keep him safe. It was in this moment, as he watched over Gabriel and Laura, his family, that he realized he'd been given the greatest gifts, trust and love.

Turn the page for a sneak peek of
SECRETS the next book in *THE OUTSIDER SERIES*
Available in print, eBook and audio

—*"Wish there were truly men in the world like the Friessen Men."*

— REVIEWER SARA

—*"This is an emotionally charged well written portrayal of a couple faced with a tragedy and the secrets that could destroy them."*

— RITA HERRON, AUTHOR

—*"The whole Friessen family show up in this story, and it was good to catch up with them all. The author really knows how to tug at your heart strings. Jed has a really tough time of it in this book, but I won't say more as I don't want to spoil the story."*

— LOVES READING

—*" This was an excellent story, emotional and tragic, with a deeply heartfelt love story.*

— MELODY

"Jed always told me he'd take care of everything. And I believed him, I trusted him, I love him."

In SECRETS, for Diana, Jed was the first man she trusted. He was the first man to show her what true love was. He was the father of her child, the one man she could always count on. Until one spring day Jed falls from the roof of the barn and Diana's world as she knows it begins to unravel.

Diana is forced to face two things, her husband's secrets, and what if... there was no Jed.

CHAPTER 1

Jed Friessen slid back the covers and slipped out of bed, his bare feet hitting the cold wood floor and rousing him further from his restlessness. He'd tossed and turned most of the night, as he had the previous night, and the night before that. The clock now ticked two in the morning, and it was pitch black outside as he stood naked, resting his arm against the bedroom window, squinting at the shadowed outline of the barn and horse paddock. Every stall in the barn was full, six horses tucked in for the night. His eyes burned as he stared into darkness, and though he could see nothing amiss, he sensed an impending darkness that just didn't sit right. He raked his hand through his sleep-tousled brown wavy hair. It was on the longish side, and even his wife, Diana, had been nagging him to get a haircut, another thing to do—something else on his plate.

A horse nickered from the barn. Another answered softly in a way that said everything was fine. Maybe they knew he was watching, wondering; Jed could still feel that something wasn't right, and he didn't know exactly what it was. Maybe it was the worry plaguing his mind that wouldn't ease. It could also be the fact he'd been working day and night for months, readying this place for Echo Springs Equine Center, the official grand opening. It would be something different from just the trail rides and pack trips. This was for Diana and her need to help others. He'd struggled past every single hurdle tossed in his path, from overpriced lumber, to his grant being yanked, to cancelled horseback riding pack trips that dried up his income stream through the summer and fall.

It was a simple dream. Diana's dream. His wife, whom he loved more than his next breath. A horse facility specializing in bringing a special needs child together with a horse, because Diana believed, as did Jed, that allowing a child with special needs to learn skills through a connection with a horse provided a different advantage from your average therapy. It didn't replace the children's much-needed therapy, but it complimented and went hand in hand with it, centering the children, bringing balance into their life. And Jed would do anything to make sure his wife's dream came true.

Diana, his redheaded beauty and the mother of his ten-month-old baby boy, Danny, lay sleeping in the small double bed. She was the most stunning woman he'd ever met, a woman who had no idea how beautiful she was. And no idea how broke they were. The thing was, Jed was determined to provide for his family, on his terms, in his way, and only with his money, which wasn't much. After breaking his leg training that young squirrelly stallion, Jed had lost the spring and some of the early summer revenue from trail rides and pack trips. That money had always been enough to set him for the winter so he wasn't living hand to mouth, and it would have helped with some of the start-up costs.

Diana had a law degree and had tried to set up a law practice in North Lakewood, but the people still didn't give her the same trust they'd given some old white-haired fart. The only thing she'd managed to pick up, work wise, was a handful of wills and minor contracts, which amounted to squat. Besides, Jed made it clear to her that he wanted Danny raised at home by his mother, not stuffed into some daycare. They were a family, and he had no intention of seeing his wife in passing as she rushed off, working on some case that would drag her from him and Danny. It was selfish on his part, and he knew it, but he also knew Diana craved a family and deep roots more than her career.

Jed had bought this ranch outside North Lakewood a few years back at auction, and for a damn good price. But then he'd had to rebuild and fix just about everything in the house, the barn, and the three cabins he used for summer guests who booked horseback riding trips each year. He wasn't wealthy, but his family was. Jed was the only son to not take a plum dime from his father. Ever since he left home, he'd had no desire to take a handout, even though his father said it was his birthright. His two brothers, Brad and Neil, and his cousin, Andy, accepted the wealth handed to them in property and money. Jed didn't begrudge them for their easy lives, but he just didn't believe he could look himself squarely in a mirror and call himself a man if he was taking money from his family. A man stood on his own two feet, made his own way in this world, and that was how Jed chose to live his life.

Even as he struggled now, he couldn't bring himself to

call his father for help, because to him that would be an admission that he had failed. So Jed had spent every spare minute turning over every rock to find the money to expand the barn, buy the extra tack, saddles, and horses, all at a bargain, thankfully. Except it had left him with nothing in his bank account and hours and hours of restless worry every night, and that was after the grant they'd been promised from the state had mysteriously disappeared. When he called the funding unit after getting the politically correct letter, they'd said funding had been cut for all areas for special needs. It was the economy, they said; but Jed learned that with governments, the first cuts always happened to the special needs, because they were the one sector of the population who didn't have the voice, the money and the time to fight back. They were and always would be an easy target. This knowledge also added to his irritation, like a sliver stuck under his nail so far that he couldn't get it out.

Jed hadn't told Diana about losing the grant. He knew she would have been crushed and would have insisted on picking up legal work, anything to help him out. Except the problem was Jed didn't believe a woman should ever support a man. That was his job, and as of late he wasn't doing so great. All they needed was cash, so as long as the students who'd signed up for the first classes next week all showed and paid in full for their six-week class, he'd have enough to pay the mortgage, buy feed for the horses and food for them. But they still needed to advertise, and there was the phone bill, medical insurance....

"Jed, what are you doing up?" Diana called out as she leaned on her elbow. The duvet slipped and exposed a hint of her creamy white breast as she sat up. She brushed back her long mussed hair with hands that brought him so much pleasure and blinked her tired, bright blue eyes. "Come back to bed."

Jed slid back under the covers and pulled her against him, running his hand down her slightly rounded belly.

Diana linked her finger with his. "Hmm, don't think I don't know you've had trouble sleeping." She rolled over and touched his cheek. "I don't need any light to see you're worried about something. What is it?"

"Go back to sleep. Just thought I heard something, is all." He brushed back her hair and kissed the tip of her nose.

"You're working too hard, but I think it's more than that. I don't need you to protect me. I need you to share what you're thinking, what you're worried about."

Jed rolled onto his back, rested his arm over his forehead, and sighed. Diana sometimes just wouldn't let things go. "It's fine, Diana. It's my job to look after you and protect you. What kind of husband would I be if I couldn't do that?" He realized too late he sounded sharp, abrupt, because next he knew, Diana sat up and slid her legs over the side of the bed.

"Diana... where are you going?" He reached over and grabbed her arm, feeling her tense up.

"Jed, I'm tired of you hiding things. And don't think I haven't noticed the stress this new horse center is putting on you. Is there something more I can do to help? What else has to be done? Maybe we should hire help."

Hire help! He couldn't believe she wanted to hire help. He ground his jaw, as that was the last thing they were going to do. "We don't need help. I'm almost done, just got to finish the roof, and then, when we start that first class next week, everything will be fine." And it would be, because the few who were interested and had signed up would be paying next week.

Diana slid around and rested her head on Jed's chest, and then her chin as she gazed up at him. "You're sure that's all?"

Jed rested his hand on the back of her head. "Next week everything will be fine. Let's get some sleep so we're not both tired tomorrow."

"I could help you get back to sleep." Diana slid her hand up his chest and drew circles with her fingernail around his nipple. She pressed a kiss into his navel, and then, trailing down, she pressed kisses lower until he pushed his head back into the pillow and felt himself sinking into a mind-blowing bliss that only Diana could give him.

She traced her fingers up his thigh and followed lower, tracing kisses to his knee and over to the other side. Jed sucked in a breath, drowning in his desire, and slid his own hands down her back, pulling her up and rolling her over onto her back.

Danny whimpered from his bedroom in their small two-bedroom home. Jed groaned. "Your timing sucks, Danny," he muttered.

Diana patted his arm to move him off her and started to get up.

"No, I'll get him" he said. "He may just need changing." Jed slid out of bed, the icy floor cooling his desire.

"Bring him back with you if he won't go back to sleep. We'll snuggle him between us. He loves that," Diana called out.

"Let's hope he goes back to sleep." Jed picked up Danny, who was now sitting in his crib, rubbing his tired eyes. "You're soaking wet." He kissed his head, his cheeks, and breathed in the fresh baby smell of his baby boy and changed him into a dry diaper and sleeper. Jed wrapped him in his blanket and sat in the rocker in the corner of the room, gently rocking him until he fell back asleep. And when Jed climbed back in bed, Diana too had fallen back to sleep. But not Jed, as he lay beside his wife, her warmth pressed against him, and he continued to worry he'd let his family down.

ABOUT THE AUTHOR

"Lorhainne Eckhart is one of my go to authors when I want a guaranteed good book. So many twists and turns, but also so much love and such a strong sense of family."

— (LORA W., REVIEWER)

New York Times & USA Today bestseller Lorhainne Eckhart is best known for writing Raw Relatable Real Romance where "Morals and family are running themes." As one fan calls her, she is the "Queen of the family saga." (aherman) writing "the ups and downs of what goes on within a family but also with some suspense, angst and of course a bit of romance thrown in for good measure." Follow

Lorhainne on Bookbub to receive alerts on New Releases and Sales and join her mailing list at LorhainneEckhart.com for her Monday Blog, all book news, giveaways and FREE reads. With over 120 books, audiobooks, and multiple series published and available at all, retailers now translated into six languages. She is a multiple recipient of the Readers' Favorite Award for Suspense and Romance, and lives in the Pacific Northwest on an island, is the mother of three, her oldest has autism and she is an advocate for never giving up on your dreams.

"Lorhainne Eckhart has this uncanny way of just hitting the spot every time with her books."

— (CAROLINE L., REVIEWER)

The O'Connells: *The O'Connells of Livingston, Montana are not your typical family. A riveting collection of stories surrounding the ups and downs of what goes on within a family but also with some suspense, angst and of course a bit of romance thrown in for good measure. "I thought I loved the Friessens, but I absolutely adore the O'Connell's. Each and every book has different genres of stories, but the one thing in common is how she is able to wrap it around the family, which is the heart of each story." (C. Logue)*

The Friessens: *An emotional big family romance series, the Friessen family siblings find their relationships tested, lay their* *hearts on the line, and discover lasting love! "Lorhainne Eckhart is one of my go to authors when I want a guaranteed good book. So many twists and turns, but also so much love and such a strong sense of family." (Lora W., Reviewer)*

The Parker Sisters: *The Parker Sisters are a close-knit family, and like any other family they have their ups and downs. Eckhart has crafted another intense family drama... "The character development is outstanding, and the emotional investment is high..." (Aherman, Reviewer)*

The McCabe Brothers: *Join the five McCabe siblings on their journeys to the dark and dangerous side of love! An intense, exhilarating collection of romantic thrillers you won't want to miss. — "Eckhart has a new series that is definitely worth the read. The queen of the family saga started this series with a spin-off of her wildly successful Friessen series." From a Readers' Favorite award—winning author and "queen of the family saga" (Aherman)*

Lorhainne loves to hear from her readers! You can connect with me at:
www.LorhainneEckhart.com
lorhainneeckhart.le@gmail.com

ALSO BY LORHAINNE ECKHART

The Outsider Series
The Forgotten Child (Brad and Emily)
A Baby and a Wedding *(An Outsider Series Short)*
Fallen Hero (Andy, Jed, and Diana)
The Search *(An Outsider Series Short)*
The Awakening (Andy and Laura)
Secrets (Jed and Diana)
Runaway (Andy and Laura)
Overdue *(An Outsider Series Short)*
The Unexpected Storm (Neil and Candy)
The Wedding (Neil and Candy)

The Friessens: A New Beginning
The Deadline (Andy and Laura)
The Price to Love (Neil and Candy)
A Different Kind of Love (Brad and Emily)
A Vow of Love, A Friessen Family Christmas

The Friessens
The Reunion
The Bloodline (Andy & Laura)
The Promise (Diana & Jed)
The Business Plan (Neil & Candy)
The Decision (Brad & Emily)
First Love (Katy)
Family First
Leave the Light On
In the Moment

In the Family
In the Silence
In the Charm
Unexpected Consequences
It Was Always You
The First Time I Saw You
Welcome to My Arms
Welcome to Boston
I'll Always Love You
Ground Rules
A Reason to Breathe
You Are My Everything
Anything For You
The Homecoming
Stay Away From My Daughter
The Bad Boy
A Place of Our Own
The Visitor
All About Devon
Long Past Dawn
How to Heal a Heart
Keep Me In Your Heart

The O'Connells
The Neighbor
The Third Call
The Secret Husband
The Quiet Day
The Commitment
The Missing Father
The Hometown Hero
Justice
The Family Secret

The Fallen O'Connell
The Return of the O'Connells
And The She Was Gone
The Stalker
The O'Connell Family Christmas
The Girl Next Door
Broken Promises
The Gatekeeper
The Hunted

The McCabe Brothers
Don't Stop Me (Vic)
Don't Catch Me (Chase)
Don't Run From Me (Aaron)
Don't Hide From Me (Luc)
Don't Leave Me (Claudia)
Out of Time

A Billy Jo McCabe Mystery
Nothing As it Seems
Hiding in Plain Sight
The Cold Case
The Trap
Above the Law
The Stranger at the Door
The Children
The Last Stand
The Charity
The Sacrifice

The Street Fighter
Finding Home

The Wilde Brothers
The One (Joe and Margaret)
The Honeymoon, A Wilde Brothers Short
Friendly Fire (Logan and Julia)
Not Quite Married, A Wilde Brothers Short
A Matter of Trust (Ben and Carrie)
The Reckoning, A Wilde Brothers Christmas
Traded (Jake)
Unforgiven (Samuel)
The Holiday Bride

Married in Montana
His Promise
Love's Promise
A Promise of Forever

The Parker Sisters
Thrill of the Chase
The Dating Game
Play Hard to Get
What We Can't Have
Go Your Own Way
A June Wedding

Kate & Walker
One Night
Edge of Night
Last Night

Walk the Right Road Series
The Choice
Lost and Found
Merkaba

Bounty
Blown Away: The Final Chapter
He Came Back

The Saved Series
Saved
Vanished
Captured

Single Titles
Loving Christine